M

I Was Howard Hughes

I Was Howard Hughes

a novel

STEVEN CARTER

A
BLOOMSBURY
TIN HOUSE
BOOK

A Bloomsbury/Tin House Book

Copyright © by Steven Carter

Published by Bloomsbury, New York and London
Distributed to the trade by Holtzbrinck Publishers

Library of Congress Cataloging-in-Publication Data has been applied for.

ISBN 1-58234-375-6

First U.S. Edition 2003

1 3 5 7 9 10 8 6 4 2

Typeset by Palimpsest Book Production Limited,
Polmont, Stirlingshire, Scotland
Printed in the United States of America by
R. R. Donnelley & Sons, Harrisonburg, Virginia

AUTHOR'S NOTE

THIS BOOK IS a work of fiction. While the information it contains concerning Howard Hughes's life and the events in his life is largely factual, all of the interviews, diary excerpts, memos, letters, and most of the quotations used are entirely fictitious.

ACKNOWLEDGMENTS

AFTER THE PUBLICATION of my first book, *Melville and the Whale*, Carol Tetley, my editor at Knopf, suggested Howard Hughes as the subject for my second book. I said thanks but no thanks. Hughes just didn't strike my fancy and, at the time, my life was topsy-turvy. I was coming off an exhausting book tour, and I was trying to finish a commissioned screenplay for *Melville*. My wife and I had just moved from Baltimore to Beverly Hills and we were still living out of boxes, eating takeout, pricing furniture, and—well, patching up some differences, let's say. There wasn't room in my life for Howard Hughes. And besides, who was he? As far as I knew, just a wealthy recluse with long hair and long fingernails who had been terrified of germs and had stayed hidden in a hotel suite in Las Vegas until he died.

But Carol kept after me, God bless her. She kept sending me old articles and clippings about Hughes. For instance, he went to Hollywood at age twenty-one and by twenty-three, he had produced a picture that won an Oscar, a comedy called *Two Arabian Knights*. The same night he won, he was discovered on a soundstage at Warner Bros., sitting on the floor in his tuxedo, the latest new movie camera disassembled into a million pieces around him; he told the guard he was just trying to see how it worked. At the same time he was making his early films he was also building what would become the fastest airplane of its day, the H-1 or *Silver Bullet*. On a Friday the thirteenth Hughes arrived at Santa Monica Airfield to pilot the plane on its first attempt at the world speed record; Amelia Earhart was also present, piloting one of the two trailing planes that monitored such attempts, and on his first run Hughes didn't try to set the record but instead played a flirty cat-and-mouse game with Earhart, dropping his plane to let her fly by and then coming up behind her. Hughes easily set the record that day, but he also ran out of fuel and had to crash-land in a beet field. He walked out of the wreck.

Old photos Carol sent of the young Hughes showed he was as good-looking as any leading man, tall, with dark hair and eyes and a shy, enigmatic smile. Women loved him, but not just for his looks. Ginger Rogers said she first felt attracted to him when he walked into the Polo Lounge wearing a tuxedo and tennis shoes. Marian Marsh said he was introduced to her at a party and said little more than hello and good-bye, but then sent her five dozen roses every day for a month. Bette Davis said she fell for him when, at a fancy Hollywood dinner party, he stood up and left the table without a word to anyone; twenty minutes later he still hadn't returned, so she went looking for him and found him in the kitchen, eating a sandwich and chatting with the servants. Errol Flynn himself gave Hughes the nickname "the Lone Wolf" as a tribute to his seemingly effortless ability to win women. A partial list of the famous women Hughes was involved with: Katharine Hepburn,

Rita Hayworth, Ava Gardner, Ida Lupino, Lana Turner, Susan Hayward, Yvonne De Carlo, Joan Fontaine, Cyd Charisse, Gina Lollobrigida, Janet Leigh, Barbara Hutton, Gene Tierney, Gloria Vanderbilt, Virginia Mayo, Marilyn Monroe, Jean Harlow.

How could I *not* want to write that man's story?

So thanks, Carol, for giving me the germ of what became a great idea.

My agent, Sherri Lollo, deserves thanks for nudging us toward contract talks and holding firm on the sum we both agreed was a reasonable figure for an advance, given *Melville and the Whale*'s surprising sales and favorable critical reception. Now, I'm going to call a spade a spade here: Knopf didn't do much to promote *Melville,* not until the grassroots groundswell among independent booksellers and the resulting sales numbers showed them they had a winner on their hands, so this time around when they balked at our asking price (let's just say seven figures), I was surprised and, as I think anyone could understand, a little miffed. But cooler heads, in this case Sherri's, prevailed, and we got the contract we wanted. In fact, thanks to Sherri's savvy and good sense everything on the business end of my career, despite gossip-column rumors to the contrary, has been going just fine.

The people who actually knew Howard Hughes and allowed me to interview them were, of course, indispensable. Some required I use their interviews in their entirety. Sometimes their reasons made sense to me—as with Jean Peters—but sometimes the demand seemed arbitrary and ill-considered. However, what's done is done, and I want to thank everyone who let me interview them.

I just mentioned Jean Peters, and I want to say more about her. During her career she was one of the most beautiful actresses in Hollywood—she looked like a young Ingrid Bergman, gorgeous, but not unapproachable. Her best-known film is probably *Three Coins in the Fountain* and it's nearly impossible to watch this romantic comedy set in Rome without falling in love with her character, a demure young woman hoping for love and a husband. She had a light touch in her acting style, nothing overdone, nothing overstated, but when she married Howard Hughes she left acting and what would've surely become a more celebrated career to devote herself to being a good spouse in what was, admittedly, a less-than-ideal marriage. However, until she spoke to me, she had never said one word to any reporter or biographer about Howard Hughes and I think that shows how much character and class she has. I feel honored she decided to speak to me, and the fact that she did, after refusing so many others, makes me believe I must be on the right track in my portrayal of Hughes. I thank her for her faith in me.

I did a lot of research at the Hughes Archives in Culver City, California, as did my assistants. There was some confusion over policy there, some misunderstandings. Neither my assistants nor I did anything wrong, and that's all there is to say.

Next, I want to thank my assistants, Jenny, Hannah, and Lois, three young women whose hard work freed me from the more tedious aspects of research. I started calling them "Alton's Angels," and though we had some laughs about that, I want each of you to know the angel part is absolutely true. Jen, I know a day didn't pass without us having one of our little spats, but just remember they never lasted long and we were usually smiling by the end of them. Hannah, I'll never eat lasagna again unless it's yours. And Lois, thanks for helping me learn to navigate Beverly Hills, in more ways than one. Each of you was a bright spot for me in the long, lonely process of writing this story. Thanks for being there.

Thanks to Lyle Peters and Tom Merkle, the craftsmen who built the replica of the Hughes box I took along on one of my research trips.

Thanks to the people at Fox Television, especially Larry Deane. Things didn't work out, but your interest, time, and financial support were much appreciated. Maybe in the future.

Next, I would like to say some things to the MacArthur Foundation. Some there have stated publicly (in a *Vanity Fair* article; in offhand "joking" remarks from the dais at the PEN/Faulkner banquet, where they ruined an otherwise lovely evening for my wife and me) that they feel I erred by not mentioning them in the acknowledgments for *Melville and the Whale*. Fine. I can go on at length about them, if that's what they want.

In *every* contact I had with *anyone* from the MacArthur Foundation I felt like I was dealing with a seventeenth-century French king handing out Christmas lagniappes. They were condescending. It was subtle, but it was there. It was the same kind of snobbery and arrogance—at heart, a cover for mediocrity—that had made me shake the dust of the academy off my feet.

Don't get me wrong. I cashed the check. I just wasn't going to bow and scrape before or after I did it. I also know enough about how awards and grants work not to take winning too seriously. The people who deserve these awards get them maybe half the time—think of the Nobel in literature. I say judge the prize by the book. Pick a decade, any decade, and get up a list of National Book Award winners. I'll jump off a bridge if you've heard of more than two of them. There's lots of politics and lots of tin ears in this world. So, MacArthur folks, please, give me a break. You didn't sweat or risk or suffer for the money you give away. You're not the writers and artists you give the money to, either, who spend years working in obscurity with nothing to sustain them but their joy in the beauty of what they've created. You're administrators. You sign checks.

Finally, and most importantly, I want to thank my wife, Alene Reece, the prettiest, smartest, kindest, most solid woman in the world. She showed unimaginable patience with me while I spent time away from her promoting *Melville* and then gadding about with Madonna and her entourage for *Rolling Stone* and then, finally, researching and writing this book. God, where has the last year and a half gone? Dear, no matter how it seems sometimes, no matter what some smiling Iago might whisper in your ear, please know that everything I do, I do for you, and even though we're back to doing the East Coast/West Coast thing after our brief "California experiment," as you call it, never doubt that you're in my thoughts every second, and if I thought my body could survive a red-eye flight to Baltimore every day I'd do it just to be with you. Someday we'll be together all the time, just like we used to be. Soon. I love you.

INTRODUCTION

HOWARD HUGHES WAS the richest man in America in the 1960s and 1970s, during Vietnam and Watergate, a time when there was a conspiracy behind every rock, and most media accounts of him from these two decades describe him as a shadowy figure using his billions to control the country through subterfuge, or they poke fun at rumors of his odd habits and appearance. Now, there's no disputing that for the last twenty years of his life Howard Hughes was troubled. He stayed isolated in a series of hotel suites in Los Angeles, Las Vegas, the Bahamas, London, Vancouver, Managua, and Acapulco, cared for (usually poorly) by a team of aides. He was emaciated—a man six feet four inches tall, at his death he barely weighed a hundred pounds—and unless he was cleaned up for the rare meeting with an outsider he kept long unwashed hair and a long beard and Mandarin-length fingernails and toenails. He was addicted to Valium and intravenously injected codeine. He rarely left his bed unless it was to use the bathroom and the last three or four years of his life he didn't get up even for that. He almost never bathed, yet he was terrified of germs—he wouldn't touch anything unless he covered his hands with several layers of Kleenex, which he called "paddles." He watched movies obsessively—when he lived in Las Vegas he bought a television station simply so he could have it run movies all night instead of signing off at 1:00 A.M. And he wrote obsessively, sometimes filling two legal pads without stopping.

This image of Hughes as an oddball hermit has stuck in our cultural consciousness to this day. However, that perception is slanted, one-sided, and just plain wrong, because even though his final years were tragic, Howard Hughes was still a great man.

In the 1920s, Hughes got his start by going to Hollywood. He knew nothing about filmmaking, and his first movie was so bad it was practically laughed off the screen at its one and only showing, but his second movie won the Oscar, and before he was thirty, he had produced *Scarface* and *The Front Page,* and he both produced and directed *Hell's Angels,* a movie about World War I fighter pilots and the first epic of the "talkie" era. It cost $4 million to make in a time when movies routinely cost under $75,000. Once, near the end of filming, Hughes wanted to get a particularly dangerous aerial dive on film but none of his pilots, some of the best in the world, would do it, so Hughes took the plane up himself. (How many directors would do that?) He waited until he was 750 feet from the ground before he tried to pull out of the dive—diving past 1,000 feet was considered impossible— and then he rode the screaming wooden biplane nose-first into the ground. To the amazement of all present he walked out of the wreck. He was taken to a hospital, where he fell into a coma, but on the third day he woke up and declared himself fine. *Hell's Angels* went on to become a success, and today film historians consider its aerial sequences some of the best ever.

Hughes had started flying when he was fourteen. One day his father took him to see the boat races at Yale and on the way home they saw a man with a seaplane anchored in the river, selling rides. Young Howard wanted to go up, but his father said his mother wouldn't like it and they drove on. However, with his characteristic determination Howard kept lobbying (for instance, when Hughes was twelve he had wanted a motorcycle but his father refused, so Hughes managed to attach a small gasoline engine to a bicycle and a photo of him riding his invention made it into the Houston newspaper); finally they turned around and went back for a fifteen-minute airplane ride. This lit a fire in Hughes, and, by the mid-1930s, he held every record of note in aviation: the airspeed record, the transcontinental record, and in 1938 he set the around-the-world record, cutting Wiley Post's time almost in half. On that flight he had the world's attention to a degree that has been equaled in our era only by the first moon shot. The radio networks carried hourly reports, newspapers published extras, reporters stayed camped outside the New York City town house of Katharine Hepburn who, it was rumored, would marry Hughes if he returned alive. When he finally landed in New York, Hughes was greeted at the airfield by a crowd of five thousand. Standing at a microphone, he mumbled a few words of thanks, gave most of the credit to his navigator and mechanic, and then, to the consternation of Mayor LaGuardia and the gathered reporters, he simply drove away in a Ford he had waiting. Two days later he was given a ticker-tape parade.

Hughes wasn't just a great pilot, though; he was also the greatest inventor of his era in aviation. He invented the retractable landing gear, the flush rivet (which made airplanes much more aerodynamically efficient) and the first oxygen-delivery system for high-altitude flights. He had a host of other more esoteric inventions only an aeronautical engineer would understand. Of course, it's fairly well known that in the 1940s he built and piloted what is still the largest airplane ever to fly, the HK-1, or "Spruce Goose" as the press called it, though Hughes always hated that name. The HK-1 was as long as a football field, with a wingspan even longer than that. Hughes started building it during World War II as a possible solution to the problem of German submarines sinking ships crossing the Atlantic with supplies and troops, but the war ended and the prototype, although on schedule, wasn't finished, and Hughes was losing money hand over fist. To most it seemed he was building an ark in the desert: the military no longer had any interest in the plane and there was no feasible commercial use for it. Hughes and his project were made a laughingstock in the newspapers and by radio comedians. However, in 1947, with a crowd of reporters present, Hughes finally flew the huge plane that no one but he, not even his engineers, thought would fly. He went a little over a mile, taking off from and landing in Long Beach Harbor.

All right. If you had any of the usual misconceptions about Howard Hughes, I hope you now see him in a new light. However, we still have to face one unpleasant question: why did such a talented and gifted man end so tragically? There are a number of possible reasons. He suffered fourteen head injuries during his life, the first in the *Hell's Angels* crash, the last from a beating he received from fifties football hero Glenn Davis for pursuing Davis's wife, actress Terry Moore. He contracted syphilis as a young man and never got rid of it completely, which caused damage to his central nervous system. He had hearing loss from a young age, the result of a rare genetic condition, otosclerosis, in which the bones in the ear continue to grow and produce a constant, maddening buzzing and ringing. After a near-fatal airplane crash in Beverly Hills in 1946, Hughes, against his will, was given morphine and codeine for his pain and developed the drug addiction that lasted until he died thirty years later. And, according to a psychological autopsy ordered by Hughes's estate, he suffered from obsessive-compulsive disorder. Of course, any *one* of these debilitating conditions would probably be enough to break a man, but I think there's another reason for Hughes's fall that's just as important as any of these. The list of Hughes's accomplishments we just examined (which just hits a few of the highlights, and doesn't even include his business successes) shows that in whatever field he entered he tried to create something bigger, better, new and original, and it seems likely that the cost of achieving these great aims contributed as much to his tragic end as any physical ailments did—Hughes finally just wore out. Physically, mentally, emotionally, and spiritually, he was spent.

Now, this isn't going to be the usual narrative biography with its birth-to-death progression and high-above-it-all analysis by the writer. This is something different, a picaresque collection of interrelated stories, interviews, memos, and letters, that, taken together, describe a hero's rise and fall. The story is divided into three sections. Just as Melville's *Moby Dick* included a section titled "Extracts," I do the same here with a collection of quotations by Howard Hughes, about Howard Hughes, and about the nature of the hero. The final two sections are called "Women" and "Odyssey," and I have used these titles for good reason. A person often has an endeavor that serves as the locus for his or her life, and if we understand that locus, we go a long way toward understanding the person. During my research I tried to identify Hughes's locus, and finally it seemed he had not one but two: his romantic relationships, and his lifetime propensity to go on extended journeys or odysseys. Of course, in examining these two areas of his life we touch on much else, such as his aviation career and his desire to build an empire in Nevada.

Hughes's story is told here through a number of voices. I often let Hughes speak for himself by printing his diary entries, memos, and letters—he was a prolific writer and a very good one, too. I interviewed people who knew Hughes, both celebrities and ordinary people, and printed the transcripts of those interviews. I used the transcripts of interviews done by Hughes biographers and since they were all twenty-five or thirty years old and had pages missing or seemed to have been haphazardly transcribed, and I had no way of retrieving the lost information, for clarity's sake I worked the material I did have into narratives to cover the gaps. I used information from newspaper articles. I took the story notes—two hundred pages of half-formed thoughts, odd details and enigmatic quotes—of a reporter who covered Hughes for thirty years, Tom Lourdes, and worked them into narratives, though in one early chapter I used two of his old interviews in their entirety. In short, what I've done is let Howard Hughes and those who knew him tell his story. When I couldn't do that, I took the material I had and created stories that told the truth about him.

That's it. I've got nothing else to say, except I hope this story is good enough to be worthy of the man it is about.

Alton Reece
Beverly Hills, California, 200–

EXTRACTS

I suppose I should have been more like other men; I was not nearly as interested in people as I should have been. But I'm not a robot, as some called me. I was merely consumed by my interest in science.

Howard Hughes, four days before his death

Whoever is on in the morning should call her at 7:30 a.m. Say that you are from Mr. Hughes's office and that we would like very much to make some photos of her and have her work with our drama coaches. Tell her that we have something coming up—a part—and we may be able to use her in it. . . . Keep her in our clutches all day. Don't tell her, but I would like to have her available so I can see her in the late afternoon. Don't tell her that I am going to see her. Tell her we'll have a car pick her up.

Howard Hughes, giving instructions to the aides he used to keep tabs on women he was interested in

I wanted some pistachio ice cream, and they weren't doing anything anyway.

Ava Gardner, recalling how she sent two Hughes aides doing surveillance on her from a car outside her house on an errand for ice cream

It is not so much the technical purity or impurity, it is the revolting, vomitous unattractiveness of the whole thing. It is sort of like serving an expensive New York cut steak in one of our showrooms and having the waiter bring the steak in to a customer in a beautiful plate, but, instead of the usual parsley and half a slice of lemon and the usual trimmings to make the steak attractive—instead of this, there is a small pile of soft shit right next to the steak. Now, maybe technically the shit does not touch the steak, but how much do you think the patron is going to enjoy eating that steak?

> *Howard Hughes, voicing fears about the*
> *possible effect of a wastewater treatment plant*
> *near Las Vegas on the city's water quality and*
> *tourism business*

Perhaps you argue that nothing worse could happen to a man? I, on the contrary, maintain that it is no bad thing to be king.

> *Telemachus in* The Odyssey, *Book I*

Although we have had reason to put into effect a program of isolation before, I want this to be ten times as effective as any we have ever set up before. With the present condition of my business affairs, which in my opinion are in a state of danger and hazard, I am sure if Jean, myself, you, or anyone else important in our organization were to acquire this disease, I just cannot even contemplate the seriousness of what the result might be. I therefore want a system of isolation with respect to Cissy [Cissy Francombe, who several years in the past had been wardrobe mistress to Jean Peters—ed.], the doctors attending her, nurses, or anyone in the past or future coming in contact with her, set up that is so effective and complete that anything we have done in the past will be nothing compared to it. I want this to go through the eighth or tenth generation, so to speak. This is one case where incrimination by association is definitely to be recognized. I consider this the most important item on the agenda, more important than our TWA crisis, our financial crisis or any of our other problems.

> *Howard Hughes's memo to an aide on the*
> *hepatitis of Cissy Francombe*

I feel that his confrontation with death after the XF-11 made him take stock of his life. And when he did, he was amazed by its emptiness.

> *Noah Dietrich, who helped Hughes run his*
> *empire for more than thirty years, commenting*
> *on Hughes's near-fatal 1946 plane crash in*
> *Beverly Hills*

He has the makings of a first-rate commercial pilot.

> *Comment on a job evaluation of Hughes*
> *when he took on a false identity to work for*
> *American Airlines*

Freud thinks the hero is always sacrificed because he is too unlike the great mass of men and therefore too threatening. His murder is usually accomplished quietly and subtly, though, his neck placed in the noose even as the crowd is applauding his exploits, and then, suddenly—bang!—the trapdoor springs and there's that terrible darkness we all dread. The hero cannot accept the inevitability of this darkness, this void, this destruction of the ego that comes with death, and according to Freud, during life he fights it by trying to gain immortality through his achievements in war, art, business, or science. Of course, while these ideas are reasonable, we must take them with a grain of salt. Freud expressed them during a time when his theories were being ridiculed.

Excerpt from Alton Reece's lecture on Freud's conception of the hero delivered at Johns Hopkins University on March 2, 1992

Nobody roots for Goliath.

Wilt Chamberlain

In university classrooms, a novel like *Moby Dick* becomes not an interesting expression of the human condition but a tedious collection of obscure symbols and indecipherable puzzles. However, heroes like Ahab and Ishmael and Queequeg are meant to be simply *experienced* at least as much as they are meant to be analyzed like a frog cut open in biology class. And don't forget Melville. He's a hero too. All writers are. Like other heroes, they make order out of chaos.

Alton Reece in the introduction to Melville and the Whale

First use six or eight thickness of Kleenex pulled one at a time from the slot in the box. Then fit them over the doorknob and open the bathroom. Please leave the bathroom door open so there will be no need to touch anything when leaving. This same sheaf of Kleenex may be employed to turn the spigots so as to obtain a good force of water.

> *Howard Hughes in a 1948 memo on how*
> *an aide was to conduct himself when running*
> *Hughes's bath*

Howard dressed like he worked for a living. Women found that very sexy.

> *Cary Grant, Hughes's friend, commenting on*
> *Hughes's usual wardrobe of a plain white shirt,*
> *workman's slacks, and tennis shoes*

. . . and why has he [textual clues in the memo, though not reproduced here, make it clear Nixon is speaking about Hughes—ed.] broken contact with us? What's happening? Why is he providing women for the Kennedys? You tell Hoover to get his ass in gear and find out what's going on. I consider this son of a bitch the most dangerous man in America.

> *Richard Nixon in an April 11, 1971, memo to*
> *Bob Haldeman, obtained through the Freedom of*
> *Information Act*

When we were filming *The Outlaw* [a 1940s western
Hughes produced and directed; it was scandalous at the time
because of the amount of cleavage Jane Russell exposed—
ed.], Howard was unhappy with the bras Jane was wearing.
Nothing suited him. Some he thought looked too pointy,
some too saggy—nothing we had would give both the
skin exposure *and* the support he wanted—so he took
matters into his own hands. He had dozens of bras brought
to him for study. He tried different types of metal wires
and cloth and fasteners and then had a model sewn to his
specifications and had Jane come in and try it on. It was a
wonderful bra.

Elton Lake, production assistant

The first half of the twentieth century was America and
Europe's golden age: despite the psychic devastation caused
by World War I, the Great Depression, the new physics
of Einstein, and the technological horrors of World War
II, it was still the last age in which bureaucracy was not
our organizing principle, men were not chained in lifelong
pigeonholes euphemistically called specialties. One doctor
delivered you and then, grizzled and wise, cut out your
tumor when you were thirty-one; quarterbacks played on
defense too; and a president, Truman, was human enough to
take strolls down Pennsylvania Avenue and we were human
enough to let him. A smart hard-working man with only a
high school education could run a corporation or edit one of
the great dailies. From Thomas Edison to William Faulkner,
Winston Churchill to John D. Rockefeller, Howard Hughes

to Humphrey Bogart—none of whom were degreed—it was
an age of genius. It was an age of giants.

> *Ellis B. Tritt, Austin Distinguished Professor of*
> *History at the University of Chicago, from his*
> *book* What Is Wrong With Us?

We had a couple of dates and I thought Howard was nice.
Joe hated him, of course.

> *Marilyn Monroe in an interview with* Screen
> Confidential, *August 17, 1955*

Dammit, Hoover, what's he [Hughes. See earlier note—ed.]
doing? It's not like we're trying to get a picture of the pope
in his bathrobe. I want some answers.

> *Richard Nixon in a May 3, 1971, memo to J.*
> *Edgar Hoover, obtained through the Freedom of*
> *Information Act*

He was like a ghost, even before those final years when
no one saw him. If he didn't want to be seen he wasn't.
You'd catch a glimpse of him and then he was gone. It was
frustrating, let me tell you, like being assigned to get an
eyewitness account of the face of God.

> *Tom Lourdes, reporter for* Screen News *and then*
> Look *magazine*

I want somebody who is an expert in the ways of animals
of this type and who would know where to look and how

to look and how to go about this line. I mean, for example, directly, dogs get a cat treed up a tree and the cat just stays there, afraid to come down, and the dogs rush around in the vicinity somewhere. . . . If we can find some evidence . . . the cat's body, or somebody who heard the episode . . . Now, it just seems to me that if Bill gave a goddamn in hell about my predicament down here he would have obtained from somewhere, someplace—I don't know where—from Los Angeles or someplace, he would have got some expert in the ways of animals, cats in particular, and had him come down here and then put about eight or ten of Maheu's men at his disposal and they would have conducted an intelligent search based upon being instructed by somebody who knows the habits and ways of an animal of this kind. But, instead of that, so far as I have been able to make out, not one thing has been done.

Kay, I am not going to run this organization this way anymore and now Bill Gay goes cruising around today, having a good time, where nothing is done about looking for this cat down here. Not one goddamned thing except having a few of our guards cruise around in their cars. Maheu is in Los Angeles. You could have had him send a team of men down here. You could have got some experts who knew about cats and know where to look. There are many, many things that could have been done during the entire period of today to try and locate this animal or find out what happened to it today. I am goddamned sure that if some police case depended upon the determination of knowledge of what happened to this animal today, by God, in Heaven, they would have had a team of men scouring the countryside and located the cat or some shred of evidence of what happened to it.

This is not the jungle; this is not the Everglades; this is not New York City with the dense population. It is thinly populated and it is no problem at all to question all the people here and have them questioned by somebody and get at the truth and not permit somebody to conceal the truth just because they are afraid of being sued or something like that.

Howard Hughes in a memo to an aide on the
disappearance of one of wife Jean Peters's cats

[The motivation for the hero's action is—ed.] . . . a strange something that derives its existence from the hinterland of man's mind. . . . It is a primordial experience which surpasses man's understanding, and to which he is therefore in danger of succumbing . . . it is foreign and cold, many-sided, demonic and grotesque. A grimly ridiculous sample of the eternal chaos . . . it bursts our human standards of value and of aesthetic form.

[The] material of the visionary creator shows certain traits that we find in the fantasies of the insane. The converse is also true; we often discover in the mental output of psychotic persons a wealth of meaning that we should expect rather from the works of a genius.

Carl Jung in Modern Man in Search of a Soul

The hero often ascends either literally in some kind of physical flight or figuratively in some kind of spiritual leaving of the body; in either case, this separates him from those of us chained to Earth by our corrupt and lacking natures. Now, this might sound funny—I'm switching gears here so stay with me—but have you ever eaten potato chips until you're sick? Even as you're doing it, you wish you weren't, because you know you're going to be bloated, sluggish, and full of self-loathing the rest of the day. You're not even tasting the chips anymore, but you still stuff your mouth until the bag is empty. Then, almost in a panic, you start eating peanut butter out of the jar with a spoon. You do that for a while. Your pants are tight, your head feels thick from hours of aimless television-watching, and you're painfully aware that you've failed yourself once again. You don't feel like you're going to be flying anywhere anytime soon. Now, how is the hero different? Well, he's able to stop eating. He has at least a modicum of faith in something beyond his immediate carnal pleasure. He's able to put that kind of mundane baseness behind him, at least sometimes. That's why heroes are rare. If you don't believe me, look at what 90 percent of television commercials are about: food, or, even if they're selling toilet paper or cell phones, sex. It makes me sick sometimes. It makes me want to go hide in Montana.

> *Excerpt from Alton Reece's lecture on the ideas*
> *of Joseph Campbell delivered at Johns Hopkins*
> *University on September 22, 1996*

This will ruin your figure and your career.

> *Howard Hughes castigating actress Terry Moore*
> *about her consumption of ice cream, cookies,*
> *and peanuts*

I found them at Terry's mother's house. He didn't try to run, he just stood in front of the piano. He didn't look scared, his face was just blank. I popped him in the chin and he fell back on the piano keys, which made a crashing musical sound. Terry and her mother were screaming, so I left. I found out the next day he had to have his jaw wired.

Glenn Davis, Heisman Trophy–winning Army end, commenting on his confrontation with Hughes when he discovered Hughes asking Terry Moore, Davis's wife of two months, to marry him

And what if the powers above do wreck me out on the wine-dark sea? I have a heart that is inured to suffering and I shall steel it to endure that too. For in my day I have had many bitter and shattering experiences in war, [love—ed.], and on the stormy seas. So let this new disaster come. It only makes one more.

Odysseus in The Odyssey, *Book V*

Well, the airplane seems to be fairly successful.

Howard Hughes just after his successful flight in the HK-1, or "Spruce Goose"

He took care of medical bills for so many people. He would read about them in the newspaper and get tears in his eyes.

Phyllis Applegate, actress and Hughes paramour, commenting on Hughes's secret philanthropy

I know what you're going to tell me. You're going to tell me, probably, that you know someone who has cancer or someone who just got married or just had a baby, and that you can't do that to those people. But don't tell me that. And I'll tell you why. Learn immediately. A corporation has no soul. I can't know about those things and be a corporation.

Howard Hughes after he bought RKO Studios, instructing an underling to fire writers

I want to be the best pilot in the world, the best movie producer in the world, the best golfer in the world, and the world's richest man. I would also like to be happily married.

Howard Hughes at age twenty-one, speaking to right-hand-man Noah Dietrich

I did not want to marry Howard. He was bright, and he was interesting. But I knew somehow that Howard and I had become friends and not lovers. Love had turned to water.

Katharine Hepburn, explaining why she rejected Hughes's marriage proposal

I grew to despise Mr. Hughes. He had no sense of fiscal reality and for many years, Hughes Tool [the oil-drill-bit company founded by Hughes's father, Howard Sr., who bought the design for a new oil drilling bit—it could cut through the hardest rock—in a saloon for one hundred dollars and parlayed it into a fortune—ed.] was the cash cow that supplied him funds to carry out his foolhardy whims. Sometimes his schemes caused us to have to cut our workforce in order to stay in business. He took food out of the mouths of our employees and their families.

> *Burton Combs, executive at Hughes Tool*
> *Company in Houston from 1946 to 1971*

In the 1960s and 1970s, it looked like Howard Hughes was getting snookered every time he made a deal. An invalid lying in a hospital bed that had become his home, Hughes, on the shaky and self-interested advice of those in his employ, bought land and mineral rights in Nevada that were little better than worthless; however, by the time his estate was finally settled, more than twenty years after his death, that formerly worthless land was worth hundreds of millions. Howard Hughes was a veritable Midas.

> *Laurence Riggs, associate professor of American*
> *Studies at Yale University, from his book*
> Luck in American History

Howard Hughes was laid to rest yesterday at Helton Memorial Gardens in a short graveside service attended by seven mourners, all distant family members.

> *Excerpt from Howard Hughes's obituary in the*
> Houston Times-Chronicle, *April 8, 1976*

I loved Howard and he loved me. I wish there was more I could've done for him.

> *Jean Peters in a 2000 interview with Alton Reece*

She'll do better than this, Odie. She'll do three-sixty-five; I
just know it.

> *The first thing Howard Hughes said after barely*
> *escaping death during a crash landing in a beet*
> *field after setting a new airspeed record for*
> *land planes*

Athene of the flashing eyes came up to him now and said:
Laertes, dearest of all my friends . . . [this is how a man wins
greatness—ed.]: quickly swing your long spear back and
let it fly.

> The Odyssey, *Book XXIV*

WOMEN

I SUPPOSE ANY DISCUSSION of a man's relationships with women begins with his mother, and most Hughes biographies make much of Hughes's relationship with his. The psychological autopsy done on Hughes called their relationship "clinging and unhealthy" (among other things, she would make him strip naked and then examine him from head to toe for signs of illness), and concluded by saying his childhood experiences with her had "marked him for life." Those kinds of psychological connections are easy to make, but they're also often sweeping, clumsy, and overstated—and I think that's the case here. What's probably most telling about Hughes's relationship with his mother is that he always spoke well of her, even in his private diaries. He never dwelled on her mistakes or blamed her for any of his problems. That says at least as much about his character as any psychological analysis could.

So, unlike every other Hughes biography I've read, in this one I respect Hughes's own understanding of his life and start his story *after* his mother's death. Over the course of the thirty years covered in this section, we see the whole arc of Hughes's romantic life. He starts out quite naïve, just trying to learn about sex, and then he tries to find his one great love and marry her; but after feeling he had found her and lost her twice in the persons of Billie Dove and Katharine Hepburn, he grows jaded, and this cynicism allows him, in midlife, to be *the* ladies' man of his generation. Then, at age fifty-two, he finally does get his heart's wish when he marries Jean Peters, a woman he truly loves; however, by this time, he's not the man he once was. He's changed, and not for the better.

You've Got to Start Somewhere

In the fall of 1925, after a honeymoon trip to Manhattan, Howard Hughes and his first wife, Houston socialite Ella Rice, arrived in Beverly Hills to set up residence. According to observers, Hughes was so shy, awkward, and distant with his wife it seemed likely the marriage had yet to be consummated; if this were true it means Hughes was probably still a virgin because our best evidence tells us he had not even dated another woman before his family arranged his engagement to Ella Rice and then pressured him to go through with the wedding.

Hughes approached learning about sex in the same methodical way he did any other subject. He read the manuals available in his day and he gained practical experience by visiting expensive prostitutes, especially those at the establishment of Sallie Donovan, which is where most of the following episode takes place.

Ethan Donovan, nephew of Sallie Donovan and as a child a resident of her bordello, reconstructed from a Hughes biographer's interview transcript
Lots of big shots came to Aunt Sallie's place and Howard Hughes was one of them, sure. I was ten when he first came around. He was always in a gray or black suit, never drank, and was

always polite. He tried to write Aunt Sallie a check the first time. Everybody laughed.

Hughes showed up every day, seven days a week, at three in the afternoon on the dot. It was a dead time in the house, with most of the girls just then getting up. Hughes'd tell Aunt Sallie which girl he wanted and wait in the parlor while the girl took a bath and got ready.

One day he spoke to me. I was carrying a model airplane through the parlor to the back porch. It was a balsa-wood model, not like these plastic kits nowadays where everything snaps together. You had to cut the wood with a jigsaw and shape the pieces by soaking them in water and putting them in clamps. The one I had that day had triple-decker wings.

"What've you got there?" he said.

I told him.

"Mind if I take a look?" he said.

I handed him the model. He held it up in front of his face and looked at it from all sides. "Pretty good," he said and handed it back. He asked me if I built a lot of models.

"Yes, sir. As many as I can," I said.

"You must like airplanes a lot," he said.

"Yes, sir," I said.

"Me too," he said. "You ever had a ride in one?"

"No, sir," I said.

"You want to go on one?" he said.

"Yes, sir. That'd be swell," I said.

"Well, I'll tell you what," he said and looked at his watch. "Go get your aunt."

He came to my house every day for six months and not one time did he ask for me.

So one day I was in the kitchen and had the needle in my arm and my nephew ran in. I could tell he wanted something but he knew better than to interrupt, so he watched me pull back the stopper and let the blood into the chamber and then shoot it back in. When I got the needle out and the tie-off undone I looked up to see what he wanted and there stood Hughes behind him, staring at me like I was an exhibit in a zoo.

"Mr. Hughes," I said.

"Does it hurt when you do that?" he said.

"No. I like it," I said.

"What kind of dope is that?" he said.

I smiled. "Would you like some?"

He shook his head. Then he said, "The boy here, I thought I might take him up in an airplane if you'd give your permission."

"Has he been bothering you?" I said.

"No, he didn't ask me to do it," Hughes said.

My colored cook walked between us and set the biscuits on the table, then went to the sink and started the water.

"I've taught him not to beg," I said. "There'll be no beggars here. He understands that." My shot was hitting me and suddenly I was in a mood to see if I could get him to ask for me. Under the table where he couldn't see I loosened the belt of my kimono and let my jugs fall out. He turned his head right away and his face got red. He kept staring at the cook.

"This boy is just such a trial," I said. "You try to teach them but they don't learn."

The cook turned off the water. "He eats more than three of them girls put together," she said.

"That's right," I said, "and he's not supposed to be in the parlor when customers are present. He knows that. Now, turn around and face me, Ethan."

I slapped him across the face. Then I pointed for him to go over and stand at the icebox.

"Mr. Hughes, would you like for me to accompany you for the afternoon?" I said.

"No," he said.

"Why not?" I asked.

"I don't like dope," he said.

"A lot of the girls use it. Surely you know that?"

He shook his head. He still wouldn't look at me.

"Most of the girls shoot between their toes so they can hide it, but I own the house so I don't have to hide it if I don't want to."

The cook finished putting away the dishes and closed the pantry door. She wiped her hands on her apron. Hughes watched her do all this. Wouldn't take his eyes off her. I found that very funny.

"Mr. Hughes?" I said.

"Yes?"

"Mr. Hughes, I'm over here," I said.

"I know where you are, Miss Donovan."

31

"Then why won't you look at me?" I said.

"Because you're not decent," he said.

"Not decent?" I lifted one of my jugs and laughed. "You're right. I'm not."

"I just wanted to know if you'd let me take the boy flying. That's all," he said.

"Doing your good deed for the day?" I said.

He shrugged. His face was as red as my nephew's where I'd slapped him.

"Go on," I said. "You think I care one way or the other? Fly to Timbuktu for all I care."

Ethan Donovan

I had to wait for him to have his encounter with the woman he'd picked that day, but then we got in his car, a big fine convertible, and took off. Down the street he pulled over and said he had to make a phone call. He went in the booth and stayed fifteen minutes. I was antsy. I just knew things weren't going to come off. Finally he came out and got in the car. "Sorry, kid," he said. "I've got some business I've got to take care of. We can't do it today."

I nodded.

"Don't worry, though," he said. "I promise you we're going flying."

I was a pretty tough kid, but on that ride back I was so disappointed my eyes watered up. I kept looking away from Hughes and he was nice enough not to say anything about me crying. He talked about airplanes.

The next morning Hughes showed up at the house, which

32

was a surprise because he hadn't said anything about us going up that morning. Nobody was awake but me and the cook. He took me to a diner for breakfast, then we went up in a two-seater biplane. He had goggles and a leather helmet and jacket for me. We went out over the ocean, up toward San Fran, everywhere. Spent two hours in the air, then landed and refueled and went up again. He let me have the controls some. Except for my kids being born, it was maybe the greatest day of my life.

I never talked to him again. He never came to Aunt Sallie's place again after he took me up. But when I was fourteen Aunt Sallie kicked me out of the house and I had to quit school and get a job, and somehow Hughes knew about it. He had a man come to my rented room and tell me he had arranged for me to live with a family in Pasadena and he gave me a part-time job as a mechanic's helper at Hughes Aircraft—after graduation, I went right into a full-time job. Then a few years later, when my wife needed an eye surgery I couldn't afford, one of his men showed up at our house and said Millie would be on a train to Johns Hopkins in two days. Understand, I hadn't mentioned her condition to anyone at work. Then when each of my three children was born there were college funds started anonymously for them at my bank and two hundred dollars was deposited every year.

Long after he had gone out of the public eye, it was 1970, a man showed up at my house right after the New Year and said he represented Howard Hughes. He said Mr. Hughes sent his best wishes and wanted to ask a favor. Did I have any family photographs I could spare? Mr. Hughes would like to see my family. By that time I was a grandfather and I'd just had a

33

couple of rolls of film from Christmas developed. I gave the man some of the prints and asked him to give Mr. Hughes my best.

After he left I sat there and thought about what had just happened and I started feeling sorry for Hughes. I had all the pictures I wanted but he had to ask me for some. Then Millie came downstairs from a nap. She asked if someone had been there, she said she thought she heard the door. I told her no, no one had been there, she was probably just dreaming. She would've been upset about me giving away her pictures of the grandchildren, but that wasn't why I lied. I wanted to keep what happened private. Between me and Hughes. I can't really say why.

That was the last time I heard from him. I would've liked to have sat down and talked with him, but of course I knew that wasn't going to happen.

Operation Nevada

In 1929, Hughes, miserable in his arranged marriage, started an affair with Billie Dove, a silent-screen star who was then one of the most popular actresses in Hollywood. She looked like the quintessential flapper, slim, coltish, with blond bobbed hair and large doelike blue eyes. They both determined to divorce their spouses so they could be together; however, Dove's husband, the director Irvin Willat, refused to grant a divorce unless Hughes paid him $325,000 (about $2.5 million today). Hughes promptly paid. Billie Dove was his first real love.

During the early, happy days of the affair, Hughes cooked up a scheme for Dove to establish residency in Nevada and obtain a divorce. The plan, named Operation Nevada by Hughes himself, called for him and Dove to masquerade as brother and sister and live together in a dirt floor lean-to as tenant workers on a small farm in Nevada. They did so for two weeks, until Hughes's lawyers discovered the lean-to was not legally a residence.

Billie Dove, reconstructed from a Hughes biographer's interview transcript

This was during the Depression and there were all sorts of transients who really were in the position we were pretending to be in. This helped make us believable. Today, because of television, something like this couldn't be done. Even an isolated farm couple like the Myersons would've known who we were and what we looked like. In those days, though, you could still get away with something like this.

Howard sprang the idea on me out of nowhere. He called up and insisted I have my maid buy clothes I wouldn't be caught dead in, but wouldn't tell me why. I got a calico dress, a bonnet, and brogan work shoes. I thought there was probably going to be a costume party. That afternoon Howard arrived in a limousine and he wore old denims, a work shirt, brogans, and a straw hat. As soon as we saw each other we started laughing. I demanded he tell me what was going on, he did and I loved the idea, and the limousine took us to the station. We boarded a coach car on a Nevada-bound train.

The Myersons were about fifty, childless, just quiet, hard-working people. During the short time we were with them Howard and I both felt guilty. Here we were playing at something that was actually survival for them. Their farm was a hardscrabble place and they made just enough to live. Howard would work in the fields all day and I would help out in the house with whatever Mrs. Myerson was doing. I learned how to can vegetables and how to kill, clean, and dress a chicken. Howard learned to plow with a mule and other things about farming. He was very interested in all of it, seemed very happy, and he didn't complain about the work. At night in the little shack that served as our quarters he would talk about what he was learning and the new ideas he had for agriculture. I'll have to say I wasn't quite as keen on it all. I had come from a middle-class background, not a farm, mind you, but I still knew about the tedium of life when you had to do all the daily things for yourself, the cooking and washing and all. I think this was the first time Howard had seen this side of life and he found it exotic.

After three days we stank to high heaven. Our shack didn't have running water and we couldn't bathe except with the pitcher and washbowl. The place had one window but it had no glass and we used a burlap sack for a covering so a lot of dust and dirt blew in. The floor was dirt. We worked in dirt all day. Everything was dirt. There were two cots and we'd scoot them together at night, though in the morning we'd have to be sure to pull them apart again in case someone came by. You'd slap your hand on the bed and enough dust to make you sneeze would bounce up. The first and only Sunday we were there the Myersons let us borrow their big washtub and we built a fire and heated water and took baths. That was quite a treat.

I guess I put up with it all because, at the time, I loved Howard and was desperate to be free from Irvin. But I lost weight while we were there, and I was pretty small to begin with. We took our meals with the Myersons and I had no taste for the food but Howard liked it, it was the kinds of things he ate anyway. A lot of fried meat, and potatoes at every meal.

In the evenings we would walk down to a grove of trees at the edge of the property where we could be alone and out of sight. We'd hold hands and talk about our future together. Howard had such dreams. In truth, most of my dreams had already come true. I was one of the most popular actresses in the movies—that was soon to end, of course, but I didn't know that then. I had all the money I'd ever need and other than a happy marriage, I had everything I wanted. Howard, on the other hand, was more restless. We would sit with our backs against a tree looking out over the miles and miles of empty land and sky and it was as if Howard was in a hurry to fill them up with something. He'd talk about his ideas for farming the desert and about building an airline that took people around the world, not just the country. He said he wanted to come to wide open places like this one and make movies with me in them. He'd go from subject to subject like a man with too many ideas in his head. He'd go on about how Nevada was just waiting for someone with his resources to move in and do things the right way and show the rest of the country what could be accomplished. He'd say we were looking at a new frontier and talk about building a new city in the desert and making it the center of the world's aviation. Ships had ruled commerce to this point in history, he would say, but now airplanes would. New York had become great because it had a great port but the city he would build in Nevada would be great because the whole sky was its port.

So he'd talk like that. Then at dark we'd go back to our little shack and Howard would light our one lamp and write in his diary until I coaxed him to bed.

Hughes diary entry, May 21, 1930
I cannot believe how well things are working out. Sometimes I am so happy I am sure somehow a fly will get in the ointment and ruin things. I will keep my fingers crossed against this and hope for the best.

I am falling in love with this state, just as surely as I am in love with Billie. I feel like I am heading out on an old time wagon train to make my fortune, as if there is a new country to be built and I am the man, or at least one of the men, to do it. Nevada is still what this whole country once was, a place where a man can break away from the past and build something new. I imagine Alaska is the same, but the climate there is too harsh to be practical.

The work here is hard but I enjoy it. My arms and shoulders are dead tired from wrestling the mule reins all day and my legs feel as if they have the arrows of St. Sebastian stuck in them but I enjoy the exhaustive nature of the work because it relaxes me mentally and is good for thinking. I have decided that the main purpose of my life, the most important purpose after my devotion to Billie, will be to build the state of Nevada into a shining example for the rest of the country and even the world to follow. It has all the necessary advantages to make this possible:

a) Hard working people.
b) Close enough to the ports of California and Oregon and Washington that, until I can design and build airships that make oceangoing ships obsolete except for recreation, we can get all the materials needed for building projects with relatively low transportation costs.
c) Oil is readily available.
d) No large cities. This will allow metropolitan areas to grow from scratch in an intelligently planned manner.
e) Low population makes the state easy to control politically and therefore the usual problems associated with government will not be a roadblock.
f) Low taxes.

Nevada will be a mecca in two areas: aviation and tourism. Right now the possibility of the growth of either in this state seems remote because it is so barren; however, that is exactly why this plan should work. This is a pie that no one except me wants a piece of. I will have a free rein here. More than likely both the regular population and those in power will be happy for the opportunities my plans offer them. I see an aviation complex growing in this state that outstrips any kind of manufacturing and services conglomerate ever envisioned. We will build the planes here, test them here, build the parts for them here, service them here, and build the world's largest and most active airfield here. As for tourism, right now I am thinking about the possibility of popularizing golf and making it the all American game instead of just recreation for the upper tier. Land costs almost nothing here and so it would be the perfect place to build golf course after golf course if I can design a cost-effective irrigation system that would be practical on this barren land. We will make golf available to the American family. Cheap enough for anyone with a decent job. We will build a string of Hughes Golf Courses across the country, with Nevada being the starting point. We will even build little courses for children with short holes and childish attractions along the way, the same way they make the little baseball gloves and bats. There will be classy hotels with swimming pools and shops and first class restaurants where families can vacation in a clean and wholesome atmosphere at a reasonable price and this growth as a tourist spot will feed our aviation business. We will attract weary city dwellers from around the country to the wholesome outdoor atmosphere of golf and we will fly them here cheaply and in style. Nevada will be an orderly state with low taxes and little or no intrusion from outside forces if a man (like me) has a good idea and wants to implement it. That is what this country started out to be but somewhere got lost along the way. Our current economic troubles bear me out on this.

I live for the day I can begin work on these plans. There are many pressures and obligations I must get rid of first, but all my problems are solvable. It will just take time and effort and I look forward to the future. Having Billie makes everything worthwhile.

Transcript of the 1930 interview between R. A. Myerson and Tom Lourdes, reporter for Screen News *and later* Look *magazine, at the Myerson farm in Tonopah, Nevada. Lourdes was the only reporter able to track down Hughes and Dove and discover the truth about Operation Nevada.*

TL: Mr. Myerson, what was your impression of Howard Hughes?

RAM: Good boy. Never shirked his work. He'd plow, hoe out a field, whatever was needed.

TL: Did you two talk much?

RAM: No, mostly we worked.

TL: You never had a conversation of any length?

RAM: Sometimes we got to talking while we was eating lunch. He'd talk about the farm. Said he was going to figure a way to put all these dry acres under cultivation, going to figure a way to put in an indoor bathtub and feed it from our well. Talked so much one day he started reminding me of one of them Wobblies. I seen them in Detroit when I worked there during the war. I asked him if he'd ever been to Detroit and he said he had and so I asked if he knew any Wobblies and he said no, he hated the Red bastards. I said that's funny cause you talk like a Wobbly. I was smiling and trying to joke him but he didn't take it like that. He got onto Hoover. Said there was a Wobbly and a Bolshevik if you wanted one. Said Hoover had made it so a man couldn't build a house or own a piece of land or start a business without getting the permission of the g.d. government. He said a man had to buy a g.d. permit to do anything nowadays.

TL: Did he talk about anything else?

RAM: He always talked about how he liked Martha's fried chicken.

Transcript of Tom Lourdes's 1930 interview with Martha Myerson

TL: Mrs. Myerson, your husband said Miss Dove seemed unhappy here, that she didn't like the work or the food and that she would start arguments with Mr. Hughes. Do you agree?

MM: Pshaw! I told him she wasn't especially good at kitchen work, but she did try. Once she started crying when she tried to bake a cake but didn't keep the oven fire hot enough and it turned out runny, but otherwise she was a fine girl to have around. And she's not a big eater, but that's her business.

TL: So you didn't think she was rude at meals?

MM: Goodness gracious no. She wouldn't take a lot on her plate when we passed the dishes. She didn't waste.

TL: What about their arguments?

MM: Well she certainly didn't start them.

TL: You're saying Mr. Hughes did?

MM: Yes.

TL: What would he do?

MM: If he wasn't trying to make her eat he was worrying her with something else. Saying he was going to do this, going to do that—all his big talk even got on my nerves so I can only guess how that poor girl felt. Then one night she said something about liking the actor in a moving picture I'd mentioned being on in town, I can't remember who it was

42

right now, and he just put down his fork and quit eating. The biscuit he had in his hand, he squeezed it into a little ball and dropped it onto his plate. R. A. asked him if the food didn't suit him. He said the food was fine but something else wasn't. That's when I knew something was funny. Brother and sister aren't jealous like that.

TL: So you believe Hughes's jealousy caused their arguments?

MM: Well, that one time. The other times it was him wanting her to eat or talking so big for so long you'd just as soon as shot him as listened to it one more second.

Alton Reece interview with Tom Lourdes at the Tremelo Retirement Home in Wharton, Vermont

I meet Tom Lourdes on a rainy Wednesday afternoon. The facility he lives in is small and dingy, though the attendants I meet seem cheerful. Susan, a slim attractive young woman with cotton-candy-pink lipstick and a habit of smiling at whatever she has just said even if it's only hello, escorts me into an empty dayroom and tells me Mr. Lourdes is finishing lunch and will be brought in shortly. She tells me that for his age, ninety-four, Mr. Lourdes is quite sharp. He's even writing a book, she says, works on it at least an hour every morning he feels up to it. I ask what the book's about and when she says Hughes, I'm surprised. Soon she leaves and I'm left alone in the room, which is much too warm and has a faint medicinal odor. The rain patters on. Finally, a wiry black man in a white smock wheels Tom Lourdes in and positions him at a round card table that has a checkerboard painted on it. Mr. Lourdes is very thin and frail—his shoulders are no wider than a clothes hanger—and he wears a faded blue terrycloth bathrobe

43

over yellow pajamas. His hair is yellowish-white and, by the smell of it, slicked down with some kind of old-fashioned barber's pomade. The attendant leaves, I sit down, and we start the interview.

AR: Thank you for seeing me, Mr. Lourdes.

TL: Oh, it's no problem. I've really been looking forward to this, and, well, I just can't tell you how happy I am to be a part of this project. Tickled to death, actually. I'm glad the truth about Howard Hughes is finally going to be made public, so that all this folderol that's usually said about him can be put to rest. That's what I've always wanted, so I'm glad we're going to be partners, I suppose you could call it, in redeeming a fine man's reputation. *(Then, with some difficulty, he bends over, flips up the footpads on his wheelchair, and places his slippered feet on the floor. He looks up, smiling wryly.)* But you know, don't you, that you're lucky I'm still alive? *(He gives a dry, brittle laugh.)*

AR: That I am, sir. *(I smile.)* Well, I guess we should get started. Wasn't the first time you covered Hughes during his affair with Billie Dove?

TL: Yes, the tabloids were saying they'd gone to Mexico for divorces, but I didn't believe it.

AR: So what happened when you found them in Nevada?

TL: Well, I actually got to talk to Hughes.

AR: Really? There's nothing about that in your notes.

TL: Yes, I asked after him with the couple on the farm, then found him sitting with Dove under some trees. She got upset, called me all manner of names. Then she stood up and looked down at Hughes and said, "I knew this wouldn't work," and walked off and left us there.

44

AR: Mr. Lourdes, I don't mean any offense, but are you absolutely certain this happened? It just seems odd you didn't write about it.

TL: No, I understand, my holding back does seem strange. I didn't— *(He starts clearing his throat and then coughing. He removes a tissue from the pocket of his robe and coughs a gob of clear phlegm into it, then shakily closes the tissue in his fist and puts it back in his pocket.)*

AR: Are you okay? Could I get you some water?

TL: No, I'm fine now, thank you. Now, as I was saying, I didn't write about actually meeting Hughes because he asked me not to. He said he was trying to work things out with his girl and didn't need any more publicity than necessary.

AR: I see. What else did you talk about?

TL: Well, we made small talk awhile . . . Oh, he wanted to know if I'd ever done a story on Greta Garbo. He kept going on about her.

AR: *(Smiling.)* A little poolroom talk?

TL: No, nothing like that. He just found her interesting.

AR: He had just convinced you to keep quiet so he could work things out with Billie Dove, so did it bother you that he asked you about another woman?

TL: *(Shaking his head.)* Not really. We were both young men.

AR: What about Hughes's wife at the time? Do you know anything about the shabby way he treated her or his frequenting of houses of ill-repute?

TL: *(Coolly.)* Young man, if you want lurid details, you don't need me.

AR: *(After an awkward pause.)* You know, I agree with you, the lurid details aren't the real story on Hughes. He's really one of our century's great figures.

TL: *(He gives a feeble, dismissive wave.)* Mr. Reece, Howard Hughes was just a simple, kindhearted man who had a very keen mind for science, and who through the accident of birth had great wealth.

(Before I can respond Susan enters the room carrying a tray with Tom Lourdes's medication. He tips a pill out of a shallow paper cup and into his mouth, drinks Sprite through a flexible straw, with difficulty swallows, and then sets the soda can back on the tray. Susan asks if on my way out I can autograph the copy of Melville and the Whale *held by the nursing home's small library, and I say I'd be happy to. She thanks me, heads for the door, and, with a final glance and smile over her shoulder, leaves.)*

AR: How old is she?

TL: *(Puzzled.)* Why do you ask?

AR: I just wondered. She doesn't look old enough to have a job like this.

TL: I believe she's twenty.

AR: You know, when she showed me in, she said you were writing a book about Hughes, too. How's that coming along?

TL: Fine, thank you.

AR: *(I smile.)* I guess we're in competition then, aren't we?

TL: *(He shrugs his shoulders.)* I don't mind a little competition.

AR: Good, me neither.

TL: We're both writing a book on Hughes. But you know, young man, there must be at least a hundred books on Hughes.

AR: Yes, you're right, there's lots of books about Hughes,

but in my opinion they've all been written by second-rate journalists. They were out of their league. In over their heads. I ran into the same thing when I researched my book on Melville, only with him it was mostly the academics who had butchered things up. *(He's no longer facing me, but instead is looking out the window next to the table and watching the rain.)* Mr. Lourdes?

TL: *(Trembling, barely audible.)* I've known some who could.

AR: What'd you mean?

TL: Reporters who could write.

AR: Oh, yes, of course. *(Realizing.)* You know, I've read a number of your old stories, and, I . . . well, the one in *Look* about *Leave It to Beaver*, I really liked that.

TL: My notes . . .

AR: Yes? What about them?

TL: You're using them?

AR: Yes, quite a bit.

TL: How?

AR: I've pieced together all the details and fragments into stories about Hughes. Those are all pretty much finished.

(For a moment he continues to stare out the window, but then he starts shaking his head. He turns to me, his brow furrowed.)

TL: You . . . you can't do that. There'd be no accuracy. You don't know what happened.

AR: Well, that's what I'm here to do today, fill in gaps. But I want to be up front with you. This book isn't even going to remotely resemble the usual narrative biography. Those things are usually just the writer's fantasy. They say more about his neuroses than they do their subject.

41

TL: I disagree.

AR: *(I smile.)* Well, reasonable people can have differences of opinion.

TL: I want my notes back.

AR: I don't have my copies with me. Also, if you recall, you signed a release for them. *(I pause.)* Say, what about this? Why don't I send you copies of the stories I built from your notes? I can't give you editorial control, but I promise I'll listen to your input. Heck, I'd like your input. It'll help. You're the expert. *(I wait for him to respond, but he just stares at me, his eyes full of confusion.)* I just want to get the story right and I could sure use your help. What'd you say? *(Finally he nods, though the movement is almost imperceptible because of his trembling.)*

TL: You have to use all of my interview. You can't edit.

AR: I'm sorry, Mr. Lourdes, but I'm not sure that's practical. I'd say you've interviewed a lot more people than I have, so you know you have to edit.

TL: I insist.

AR: Well . . . *(I sigh, then turn off the tape recorder.)*

Howard and Greta Garbo

Greta Garbo letter to Howard Hughes, dated September 8, 1930

Dearest Howard,

Will you please reconsider and at least, <u>at least</u>, think about moving? Valence is a wonderful little city and we could have a beautiful life there. I know you would love France.

48

I would do almost anything to be with you, except be in another movie. Please don't ask me to do that. That is the one and only request I will ever make of you, my big Howard. I know you can make a wonderful movie without me, though I will be jealous of the lucky actresses who get to spend all that time with you. I will check you each day when you come home to make sure I don't smell the least little bit of perfume!!!

I will see you next week.

Greta

Hughes diary entry, September 21, 1930
Greta's great, but she's a clinger. I'm not sure what to do.

Howard and Kate

Howard Hughes had a very public romance with Katharine Hepburn in the 1930s. He wanted desperately to marry her and she spurned him, but the following diary entries date from the time before the couple split.

Hughes diary entry, August 11, 1937
Arrived Kate's parents' house tonight. The Sikorsky [Hughes's seaplane—ed.] did okay on the flight in, though during the last thirty minutes it sounded like there might be a valve problem developing again.

No one met me when I arrived except Kate. Her parents were at a dinner party at Ludlow's [Ludlow Stevens, Hepburn's ex-husband—ed.]. I knew they were still close with this man but if he is around much I don't know how I will handle it.

Kate seemed preoccupied and distant. We sat in a room that

has big windows and is on the ocean side of the house. The windows were all wide open the way she likes them. I could feel the grit on the breeze from the salt air. It bothered me. Kate was reading a magazine and I was just sitting there watching her. I asked her what was wrong. She said nothing was wrong. I said she didn't seem like herself. She asked what herself was. I said forget it. She apologized but offered no explanation. Then I asked her if Ludlow was going to be around much during my visit.

Probably she said. You know he is still quite close with Mother and Father.

I do not take it as a good sign that her parents weren't here when I arrived, but were at the ex-husband's. I suppose that is actually a terrible sign.

Hughes diary entry, August 12, 1937

Ludlow was at breakfast this morning when I came down, Kate and her parents too. When I walked in they were all laughing but stopped.

Howard this is Ludlow Kate said. And my parents, such as they are.

I gave Ludlow my hand and said hello. He said Howard and smiled in a smart ass way. He was much shorter than I had expected. I sat down next to Kate. Her mother had a smile that looked like she had a fly in her mouth at a White House dinner and did not want anyone to know it. Her father did not even pretend. He just nodded, then picked up *The New York Times* [italics mine].

We are so happy you are here her mother said.

I am back. Dinner was about the same as breakfast only it went on longer. I could not understand a thing anyone said because there was too much chatter and people were chewing so I could not read their lips. I am going to have to find a top-notch doctor to do something about this hearing ordeal.

The only thing that really bothers me about the cold shoulder I am getting from these people is that it does not seem like Kate is taking up for me. If I had any family left for her to see, if my dear mother and father were still living, I would not let anyone give her ill treatment of any sort. I understand she is in an awkward position and that these people see things differently than I do. With them everything is droll.

We played golf this afternoon. Ludlow had one of these new handheld home movie cameras and several times when I was standing over my drive or getting ready to putt I would look up to see that pumpkin ass pointing the camera at me. The first time it happened was on the tee at the second and I stood there staring into the camera astounded. I had never seen such a thing among golfers. I waited. Her father was smiling. Kate said Go on Howard. It is just Ludlow being Ludlow.

Please stop I said. It is distracting.

He did not stop.

I said please stop I said.

Then her father said the most words he had said to me to that point. He said Howard Ludlow is part of our family, has been for a long time and will be for a long time after you are gone. He takes pictures of us all the time. So go ahead and play. I think you are using the wrong club for this shot, by the way. Try a five.

I was furious. I drove using the club I had, a seven, and the ball landed six feet from the pin. I finished in two.

These are people who go on birthright and place of education, like Harvard or Princeton or some such place as that, instead of what a man can achieve with his own intelligence and determination. If you put Ludlow in a cockpit I do not think he would have enough nerve to piss his pants. He works in his father's stock firm and will never do anything other than that except waddle around a golf course on his fat ass after me and Kate when we come to visit here, which I hope is not too often. Her father is a doctor and I will give him that. It takes some nerve to slice open a living gut.

By the 18th I was tied with her father. We were both on the green in three, but I had a better lie. He putted first and ended up with a twenty footer for his second putt. Of course, Ludlow filmed none of this. He never filmed Mr. Hepburn but often filmed Kate and she played up to it. She skipped around like a damn elf. On his second putt her father got within four feet and then it was my turn. I stood over the ball, then looked up and saw Ludlow filming.

I butchered the putt on purpose. I hit it long and there was a hill past the hole and I knew the ball would roll down it. I would three putt up this hill and he would win by one stroke. I hoped that would make him more friendly.

When my ball rolled too fast by the hole and started down the hill Ludlow almost skipped to keep up with it, the camera pointed at the ball. I guess watching that film will be a comfort to him while I am watching his former wife change clothes the rest of my life.

Good round I told Mr. Hepburn when we were finished.
We both played well he said.

Kate came up and stood by my side and put her arm around
my waist and hugged me—from the look on her face I was
pretty sure she knew I had let him win.

I have decided not to eat with them anymore. I am just not
putting myself through that.

Hughes diary entry, August 14, 1937
They played golf today but I did not go. Kate wanted me to
play but I wanted her to stay with me. We argued and she left.
I got the cook to pack a lunch, then went down to the dock
to work on the Sikorsky. I got the valve problem straightened
out and then took off.

I spotted them on the 11th, a par three too short to land
on. I came in low and tipped my wings, then circled until
they were at the 14th, a par five with four hundred yards of
fairway until a dogleg a hundred yards from the green. I started
my approach as Ludlow teed up and then pancaked the airplane
down, bouncing down the fairway until I stopped right at the
dogleg. Another five yards and I would have crashed into the
woods. Some bluebloods in a cart had to make a run for it
to get out of the way. As soon as I stopped they headed back
toward me. I cut the engines and opened the cockpit window.
What in hell do you think you are doing? one of them said. I
told him I had to make an emergency landing. There is nothing
wrong with this airplane he said. Your engines were running
just swell.

Ludlow, Kate and her father were coming toward us in their

cart. The landing had torn up the fairway. Chunks of turf made a trail all the way to the plane.

Who in hell do you think you are? the man said. This is private property, a private club. I apologized and said I would pay to repair the fairway and would also pay his party's green fees for the day.

What's your name? he said. He kept looking for his scoring pencil but could not find it. Do not think you are getting away with this he said. I told him his pencil was behind his ear and then told him I was Howard Hughes. All of them looked at me closely. You are not Howard Hughes the man said. Yes I am I said. Can you prove it? he said. I jerked my thumb back down the fairway. I just did I said.

Kate pulled up. She was laughing. Her father and Ludlow looked angry. She came up below my window. Did you have a problem? she asked. Why did you land? My God, what a landing! My heart was in my throat!

I have a picnic lunch for us I said. We can go over to that pond by the 8th tee.

Howard! she said. For goodness sake.

Mr. Hughes, get this goddamned plane off the golf course her father said.

Do not think you have heard the end of this the man said. What you have done is serious. You endangered lives.

I did not say anything. I smiled at Kate.

There was not enough fairway for a takeoff so I taxied the plane as much out of the way as I could. Kate walked with me to the pond at the 8th and we ate. Later I arranged to have the Sikorsky partly disassembled and transported to a hangar for reassembly. This will cost only five thousand. I was expecting ten.

Hughes diary entry, August 16, 1937
Got caught alone in the dining room this afternoon with Kate's father. I waited until I thought they had all cleared out from lunch and went down for a sandwich. Her father walked in carrying a glass of lemonade. He smiled and sat down.

I see we have driven you to ham sandwiches and cold coffee he said. Next thing you will be eating in the kitchen with the cook.

I have been feeling ill the last few days I said. Maybe a touch of food poisoning.

You do not have food poisoning Howard. Remember, I am a doctor.

Yes. Well, it has been something else I suppose.

He closed his eyes and rubbed the bridge of his nose. He did not speak for a long time. I continued eating.

I am dying he said.

Excuse me?

I am dying. He opened his eyes.

You seem the picture of health I said but immediately wondered if it was something I could contract.

I have inoperable liver cancer he said.

I am very sorry I said.

Yes I am too he said. Do you believe in an afterlife?

I certainly hope for one I said.

Yes I do too. If there is not one I am going to be one angry son of a bitch.

Kate did not tell me about this I said.

Kate does not know. No one knows. I am going to keep it from them as long as I can.

I understand.

Why I have told you I do not know. I think I sensed you are man enough to keep your mouth shut and I have been feeling the weight of this and wanted to tell someone. I wanted to talk to someone who would not panic.

I will not speak about this to anyone. You have my word.

Let me ask you something he said. If you don't mind, I am just wondering. Are you a reader?

Yes. I suppose I am.

What do you read?

Mostly aviation and technical manuals, things of that sort. Anything in the sciences.

For the most part I have stuck with the sciences too he said. But my wife is a great reader of literature and over the years I have picked up a book of hers here and there. One especially became a favorite of mine, a book of Anglo Saxon poetry. Did you happen to read any of that in school?

Not that I recall I said.

One of the poems has always stayed with me he said. I can quote parts of it I have read it so many times. It was in the same manuscript as the *Beowulf* [italics mine] poem. Did you read *Beowulf* [italics mine] in school?

No but I was supposed to I said.

The poem I like is about Vikings landing in England in the tenth century at the village of Maldon. The Vikings demand gold but the leader of the village, an old man who can barely fight anymore, refuses and the two groups begin fighting. The old leader gets injured right away but does not die. Some of his men run away when they see the battle is hopeless, but some form a circle around the fallen old man, shoulder to shoulder, and even though they know they are dead men if they stay, they keep fighting. The old man says aim shall be the harder, heart the keener, manhood the more, as our might lessens.

That sounds like a good poem I said.

Yes but now that I am dying like that old man I do not like that poem nearly so much as I always did. I think I actually hate that poem. Do you understand what I am saying?

Yes.

There is one more thing he said. These are my dying words to you, like that old man's. Break with Kate. Will you grant me that one wish?

I cannot do that I said. I am sorry for your illness and I am sorry you do not approve of me and Kate. But I love her and want to marry her.

I do not dislike you Howard he said. I can understand why you would think that. We have treated you shabbily while you have been here. But I actually like you. I will be honest with you, my wife does not care for you. Ludlow is a vacuous tart, I know that, but I believe he is what Kate needs. You are too much like Kate for you two to ever get along. You both are headstrong people who love being in the limelight. That is not a good formula for success in marriage. People in a marriage have to be willing to give up some of what they want and neither of you is like that. But Ludlow is willing to give up anything for Kate.

I realized it did not make any difference what I told him, he was dying. I did not have to stick to anything.

I see the truth of what you are saying I said. You are probably right about me and Kate. I will step aside, but I will do it slowly if that is all right with you.

He grabbed my hand in both of his. Yes, that is fine. Thank you, thank you so much. Please, Howard, eat with us this evening. We are having rock lobster.

Hughes diary entry, September 11, 1937
Today I came home from the aircraft plant thinking I ought to tell Kate about her father's illness since I had never liked the fact I had not been told my mother was going into the hospital and then she was gone, so when I got home I sat Kate down on the bed and held her hand and told her about her father. She said I cannot believe this, this is the third time he has told this liver cancer story to men I have brought to visit.

I was angry about being made a dupe but I told her it was not her fault.

Later at dinner I asked her who the other two men were who were told this same story.

It does not matter she said. I am so angry at Father I just do not want to talk about it.

I am just curious. Just tell me.

I said I do not want to she said.

Look. I have put up with a lot from your family and have been very good-natured so I do not think this is too much to ask.

You are only asking because you want a reason to be jealous.

I am not going to pander to that part of your personality. There is absolutely no good reason to mention who it was.

Was Ronald Colman one of them?

This discussion is over. She put a bite into her mouth. I looked at my plate. The beef chunks were irregular and the rice kernels were tiny runtish things. I yelled for Linton. Kate asked what was wrong.

There's a hair in my beef tips I said.

Yuck she said and wrinkled up her nose.

Linton came and took our plates away. I told him to bring me two chicken sandwiches, a Hershey's bar, and milk. Kate said she did not want anything else. Then she got up and went to the bathroom.

That part of my personality kiss my ass. Why did she drag me into that hellhole without warning me I might be lied to? Maybe she warned the others and not me. I will never know about that though because I have to rely on her for the truth. The idea that any truth exists outside of mathematics and chemistry and aerodynamics and the engineering sciences is absolutely and utterly insane and even the truth in those areas is constantly changing. Truth is a lie for women and children and weak men to believe so they do not get discouraged. A man can know there is no truth and keep going but he still hopes his girlfriend is not a liar. But there are always secrets and you can never know when you are being lied to or when a woman is going to change her mind about loving you, and it has nothing to do with you, but is just her whim like it happened with Billie [Dove—ed.]. Without warning you are alone. Or it rains, a car skids, and she is killed, like with Sarah [Sarah Elway, a favorite prostitute of Hughes's who was killed in a car accident during his early days in California—ed.]. Or an unseen germ descends and she dies like with Mother. Kate thinks I am jealous but I am actually just one of those unlucky people who cannot put these awful realities out of my mind and tell myself lies that cover them up day in day out. I understand the importance of preparing for every eventuality and putting all the resources of your organization behind your efforts. I suppose this is why people become priests because they cannot put these realities out of their minds either and they do not have the resources I do to take care of things so they just go all out on the religion business hoping there is another world with more order than this one.

Who would not want to know who those two men were? A simple speaking of their names would put everything to rest but I guess that would be too easy and she would not have anything to smile about for the next three days.

A Gift Is A Gift

Following his breakup with Katharine Hepburn, Hughes was heartbroken. It seemed conventional ways of conducting romance weren't working for him, so he tried a different approach and for the next twenty years he always had one primary relationship (here it is with the young, unknown actress Faith Domergue) and several secondary relationships (here they are with Ava Gardner and Lana Turner). It seems he wanted to make sure he didn't get left completely alone again as he did when Billie Dove and Katharine Hepburn left him.

Hughes diary entry, November 3, 1946

For those who study my life after I am gone, the biographers and reporters and possibly even historians, all the soul-murdering bastards whose opinions will create my legacy no matter what I do for this country, for those who are reading this diary entry in whatever year 2020 or whatever, I say this to you, there are people in this world who will cut your finger off, then cut your hand off, then cut your arm at the elbow, then take the whole arm from the shoulder, and the whole time they are smiling, they are your friend, and you don't know they really aren't your friend until your arm is gone and you are standing there bleeding, with blood spurting from your shoulder and torn muscles hanging like untied shoelaces and your screams drowning out every other noise and for history I want it known that Ava Gardner is one of the people who starts cutting and doesn't stop. I want it on record. See if you can get this one thing right. Just copy it off this page onto yours: AVA GARDNER WILL CUT YOU ALL THE WAY.

She calls and says she wants her Mercedes back. I'm thinking what Mercedes and when I don't say anything she says the gray Mercedes I gave her three years ago that she gave back when she married Artie Shaw. Now that she's not with little Artie she wants it back. I told her it'd been here so long I thought it was mine, but sure, she was welcome to it, a gift is a gift.

The day after her call I receive the daily observation logs from Munson. I read through Faith's pages, Lana's, Rita's [Rita Hayworth—ed.], several others, and everything's in order everywhere, nobody going behind my back with someone I didn't know about before, until I read Ava's. I'm copying it here so you goddamn journalists a hundred years from now won't have to try to find it because if everything goes according to plan the original will be destroyed.

Ava Gardner, Friday, October 11, 1946

7:00 am	*no activity, presumed asleep*
8:00 am	*no activity, presumed asleep*
9:00 am	*no activity, presumed asleep*
9:53 am	*leaves apartment in company of chauffeur*
10:07 am	*picks up agent*
10:34 am	*arrives studio, goes with agent to meeting*
11:00 am	*out of sight, presumed in meeting*
12:00 pm	*out of sight, presumed in meeting*
12:46 pm	*arrives Beverly Hills Hotel, eats lunch with agent and unknown woman*
1:00 pm	*lunch*
2:00 pm	*lunch*
2:49 pm	*drops off agent*
3:02 pm	*arrives back at apartment, stumbles on sidewalk, falls, tears hose, curses loudly, chauffeur has to use key for her, she's drunk*
3:17 pm	*Howard Duff arrives*
3:26 pm	*They enter bathhouse fully clothed*
4:18 pm	*They emerge from bathhouse in bathing suits, Miss Gardner in a white two-piece*
4:19 pm	*They swim* [all italics mine]

The son of a bitch didn't*** [In the rest of this paragraph, the text is corrupted beyond recognition by a large, dark, irregularly shaped stain—ed.]

I called the aircraft plant and got Russelli and Tompkins sent out to the house. They arrived around noon and I sent them out to the garage where the Mercedes was. I had a table set up with chicken sandwiches, apples, chocolate bars, milk. I told them to wait on me for instructions. I told them not to touch the food until I got there.

Faith was in the kitchen. She had silver mixing bowls everywhere, two ovens going, flour all over herself. It was just the two of us but with the mess and the heat from the ovens it seemed crowded and tight like a subway station back east and as soon as I walked in there I felt like I couldn't move without hitting something. I sat down.

Whatcha doing? she said.

Nothing. What's cooking?

A cake.

Looks like you're feeding an army.

Very funny.

What kind of cake?

Cherry chocolate. What're you guys doing this afternoon?

I looked out the window at the driveway and the hill that leads up from the road, where the cars passing looked slow because they were so far away. I unbuttoned the top of my shirt. I was sweating.

We're working on a car I said. I wanted to talk to you about it. Ava Gardner is going to be here this afternoon. I didn't want you getting upset, but she's coming for this car, a Mercedes. I'm getting it ready for her. It's a long story but it's hers, she's taking it, and then getting the hell out of our lives completely.

Is she coming in?

No. God, no. She's just getting the car and going.

Well, if she does come in here I don't want to see her. Keep her away from me, Howard.

Don't worry. How'd you get flour on the tip of your nose, my little cook?

I went upstairs and changed into a dry shirt, then went out to the garage, where Russelli and Tompkins were arguing. Tompkins has no teeth and won't wear the false ones so when he talks I can't understand him. It's different lipreading someone with no teeth, like a whole other language.

What is it, boys? I said.

Mwah mwah Tompkins said. [This is the only instance of onomatopoeia in the thousands of pages of Hughes's writings that my assistants and I reviewed—ed.]

I looked at Russelli.

I did not he said. That's crazy.

We sat on a workbench and ate. I was between Russelli and Tompkins. Tompkins's legs were dangling like a kid's. The milk bottles were cold and sweaty. I rubbed mine on my forehead and got ice from the bucket and rubbed my arms.

So what are we doing today Boss Russelli said.

We're going to make some changes to that gray Mercedes over there. We're going to loosen a number of parts. The muffler, things like that. I'll show you.

What for?

Because Ava Gardner is going to pick it up this afternoon.

I don't get it.

She's a two-timer I said.

Oh, sorry to hear that Boss.

Then the door from the house to the garage opened and it was Faith, so much flour on her she looked like a damn geisha.

Howard, you've got a telephone call.

Who is it?

It's her she said and she nodded at the Mercedes.

Just go back and hang up the phone. Just hang it up without another word.

I don't want to do that.

Why not?

It seems strange.

Then leave it off the hook.

She left. There was a white handprint on the door where she touched it.

We loosened the muffler, the driver side mirror, the bolts that hold the universal, the timing chain, and many other things. It was a delicate operation because whatever we were working on had to be loosened just enough that she could drive a short distance down the hill from the house before it fell off. The parts had to fall off one after the other like in a cartoon so she would realize what a fool she was for betraying me. We didn't screw with the brakes or anything that would cause an accident. I didn't want her to die, I just wanted to see her face through the binoculars while things fell off. It was tricky getting everything right. Turning this nut or that one just the right number of turns so its falling off corresponded with precisely the correct distance she would travel down the hill. Mercedes automobiles have a low vibration quotient either idling or moving and that had to be taken into account. Mercedes is a helluva car. Germans. One thing the journalists a hundred years from now will probably conveniently forget when writing the Howard Hughes story is that in the past six months I have saved a number of German scientists from falling into the clutches of the Communists. They're at Hughes Aircraft right now twiddling their goddamn thumbs and living in paradise instead of freezing their asses off in Moscow and designing weapons to destroy America. . . . [In the text that finishes this paragraph, several passages have been blacked out, just as a censor would do. We can only assume Hughes did this himself, because according to the curator of the Hughes Archives this particular diary had not been reviewed before I read it, and we know that during his lifetime Hughes closely guarded his diaries. I reproduce the passage here by substituting xs for portions of the text that have been blacked out—ed.]

xxxxxxxxxxxxxxxxxxxxxxxxxxxxxxxxxxxxxxxxxxx xxxxxxxxxxxxxxxxx the Berlin question xxxxxxxx xxxxxxxxxxxxxxxx the Senate does not have the will xxxxxxxxxxxxxxxxxxxxxxxxxxxxxxxxxxxxxxxxxxx and in his more lucid moments, Dewey knows that xxxxxxx xxxxxxxxxxxxxxxxxxxxxxxxxxx believe Truman xxxxx xxxxxxxxxxxxxxxxxxxx she's just a lying, miserable bitc xxxxxxxxxxxxxxxxxxxxxxxxxxxxxxxxxxxxxxxxxxxx xxxxxxxxxxxxxxxxxxxxxxxxxx and yet Malaysia is probably the best staging area of all for xxxxxxxxxxxxxxxxxxxx xxxxxxxxxxx

I put the car in neutral and steered it out of the garage into the driveway while Russelli and Tompkins pushed. We wanted as little jarring to the car as possible. Our calculations had been precise. They pushed me into the drive and up to the front door. I stepped on the park brake, took a rag and wiped the grease off the steering wheel, and then we sat on the stone bench near the front door. I remembered the binocs and told Tompkins to go to the garage and get them. He came back with them hanging from his neck and they damn near reached his knees. He had an apple he had been eating earlier. The white part had turned brown.

When Ava arrived Duff was with her. They drove up behind the Mercedes, right in front of our bench. I couldn't believe the nerve. Ava had her window down smoking. I stood up.

The keys are in the ignition I said.

What're you doing with those binoculars? she said.

Nothing.

She frowned. Why wouldn't you talk to me?

Hey Duff said. Did you call him?

You were in the shower.

Look, just get your car and go Ava I said.

She opened the door and got out and then got into the Mercedes. I went over and leaned into the window. She pulled the choke.

It's not too late for us I said.

Please don't she said.

I love you. I'll do anything for you. I'll give you anything.

Do you know why I called you?

Yes, it was because you want us to be together again.

She twisted the rearview mirror so she could see herself and started patting her hair. It was because you have to stop sending

67

flowers every day she said. Howard got so angry this morning he threatened to put a contract on your life.

Screw him. I'll risk death for you.

No more flowers. I'm refusing delivery from now on.

I can't believe you're so coldly throwing away all we had.

She stopped looking at herself, readjusted the mirror, and put her hand on the ignition.

Don't start this car I said.

Do you know Faith is watching us? She's watching out those windows over there. You stand here and say these things as the woman you live with watches and you don't even know it.

Yes I do.

Then that's even worse. She turned the ignition. It didn't start. Did you do something to this car? she said.

Give it more choke I said.

She did and it fired right up. She put it in gear and started around the driveway and Duff pulled out behind her.

I went back to the bench and sat down. I lifted the binocs and watched. She wasn't thirty yards down the hill when the muffler fell off, then right after that a flywheel popped out. Her mouth looked shocked and ugly. More stuff fell off. Duff had to swerve to miss each part as it popped out from under the car and bounced on the road. Ava stopped halfway down the hill and Duff stopped behind her. They got out. They looked behind them at the car parts in the road. They argued. Then Duff got her into the car and they drove off.

I lowered the binocs. Get that thing back up here I said. Put it back together and then put everything back in order in the garage. But get that grease off of you before you touch that car or anything in the garage. Use the hose out back. Then take the hose and put it in your truck. Take it with you when you leave and destroy it at the plant. Put it in the incinerator. I'm going to call security and make sure you did that. Understand?

Sure thing Boss.

Good day's work boys.

Alton Reece interview with Faith Domergue at her home in Palo Alto, California

Faith Domergue lives in a small bungalow in a middle-class neighborhood where most of the houses show their age, except for hers, with its manicured yard and recently painted stucco. I arrive on a Sunday afternoon at our appointed meeting time, but she's not home, so I park in her driveway, lower the windows, and turn on the radio.

Faith Domergue's story is a fairly common one from the days of Hollywood's studio system. Though she had little acting experience, Warner Bros. Studios, on the basis of her looks alone, signed her to a contract when she was fifteen. Her parents were Spanish and French and she was a small, slim girl with dark hair, olive skin, and strikingly beautiful eyes. Hughes met her not long after she signed with Warner Bros., at a party he was hosting for the studio on his yacht. He and Domergue immediately fell for each other, though he was more than twice her age, and less than a week later Hughes had purchased her contract from Jack Warner for fifty thousand dollars. She and Hughes began living together two months later, with her parents and siblings installed in a house nearby. Hughes arranged drama, dance, and golf lessons for her, bought her a stylish new wardrobe, and supplied tutors so she could finish her education. She didn't appear in a movie, though, until 1950, two years after her breakup with Hughes. Over the next few years she found occasional roles, then gave up acting.

Faith Domergue finally arrives, forty minutes late. I wave, and she blows the horn and motions at me: she wants me to back out of her driveway so she won't block me in. I move my car, she pulls her silver Taurus up into the drive, and I pull in behind her. She gets out. Her gray hair is pulled back into a bun, she's wearing a high-necked, dark blue dress, and she's plump and matronly, no longer the wisp she was when young. She explains that Mass ran late and then traffic was bad. Then she stands beside my car a moment, looking it over, and says she's been thinking of getting a Lexus herself, a used one. She asks me how I like mine. I tell her I've had it just two weeks, but so far I like it fine.

Inside, while she changes clothes, I stand in her living room and examine a wall of photographs above the couch, the typical shots of family and friends. There's only one from her days in Hollywood, it's black-and-white and she's reclining on a dark couch, wearing a sequined, low-cut evening gown, her legs are curled under her, and she stares directly at the camera with the sultry look typical of 1940s publicity shots.

She returns wearing a powder-blue pantsuit, and we move to the kitchen, dark, cool, and smelling faintly of cabbage. She puts coffee down for both of us.

AR: Ms. Domergue, thank you very much for agreeing to see me. *(She nods.)* My assistant said you wanted this interview to be recorded word for word in the book so you wouldn't be misquoted. I understand your concerns and doing things that way is fine. *(She nods again. Though earlier she seemed relaxed enough, now that the interview has started her manner is hesitant, nervous. She takes a sip of her coffee, and I notice her hand is trembling—she catches me watching her hand and quickly looks away, embarrassed. There's an awkward silence. The ticking of a grandfather clock in the living room is the only sound in the house. When she finally looks at me again, I smile to try to put her at ease.)* Well, Ms. Domergue, I guess we should get started. *(I glance at my notepad.)* You were quite young when you and Hughes became a couple. Any comment on that?

FD: Well, if we had gotten together today, in this day and age, Howard would have been arrested.

AR: So despite the sexual revolution, we've actually grown more provincial—I've recently been thinking the same thing. I was in Europe earlier this year promoting a book and cultures there seemed much more open and accepting about different-age relationships.

FD: *(She sighs audibly.)* I'm not saying it's a good idea for a high-school girl to live with a forty-year-old man. I'm just saying that's just how it happened for Howard and me.

AR: So how did he win you?

FD: Well, he bought a house for us to live in, even though I hadn't said I'd move in with him, so that led me to believe he was serious about me, serious about us. The day he took me over to see it, he'd had the foyer filled with yellow roses, my favorite flower. It was a huge foyer with a cathedral ceiling and there were literally thousands of yellow roses. It was unbelievable. Those flowers must've cost three or four thousand dollars. That was at least a year's salary for my father. *(She pauses. The color in her face is high; when she speaks again her voice is low and lilting.)* That day was the first time we had relations.

AR: Well. *(Awkward silence.)* So what was life together like?

FD: Strange. Howard saw a lot of other women.

AR: And that bothered you?

FD: *(Defensive.)* What'd you think?

AR: Well, some people have open relationships and are happy with that . . . I mean, they understand that their partner is just a very vital person with a lot of—what should I call it?— libido energy—and they accept that about him.

FD: How many people really live like that?

AR: I don't know. I'm just speaking hypothetically.

FD: I put up with it because I was young and didn't know any better. I also had my family to consider. My father and uncle had been given good jobs at Hughes Aircraft. I wasn't sure either what would happen to my acting career. Howard owned my contract. He knew everyone in Hollywood.

AR: So you felt trapped. Did you resent Hughes?

FD: *(She looks down and wipes imaginary crumbs from the table, which is already as clean as a pin.)* Yes.

AR: Do you still?

FD: *(With barely disguised anger.)* Of course not. Not now.

AR: So what finally caused you and Hughes to break up?

FD: Things just fell apart.

AR: For instance?

FD: Oh, Howard was going after more women than ever, but he also was having me monitored more closely than ever. A man was always following me, staring right at me like I was a fly he was trying to kill. Howard was staying gone for days, too, with no explanation when he came back. He never took me with him, but he was always saying someday soon we were going to be together all the time. Of course, it never happened. He valued other things more than he did me.

AR: Well, there are a lot of different parts of life and work is one of them. Sometimes we go through periods where we have to spend more time on one thing than on another.

FD: Yes, but you still have to make choices. I believe you can tell where someone's treasure is by where they put their heart, and I was never Howard's treasure. His work and being in the public eye, that's where his heart was, and you see how he ended up.

(I accidentally knock over my cup and coffee spreads in a dark puddle across the table. I quickly move my recorder away from the puddle.)

AR: Sorry, sorry. *(I get up from the table and come back with paper towels and spread them over the spill.)* Sounds like you're saying something along the lines of leopards have spots and there's nothing they can do about them. He wasn't going to turn out well no matter what.

FD: I suppose.

AR: *(I gather the sopping paper towels into a wad and she directs me to the garbage pail underneath the sink. I return to the table and sit down.)* Of course, you knew Hughes much better than I do, I didn't actually know him at all, but what you just said, as a general comment about human nature, the human condition, I'd have to disagree with that. I think it's possible to equally value two or three things at the same time and to value them all dearly. Whether it's your work and another person, or even two or three people you value equally, it doesn't mean you don't love them all. Monogamy is really an illusion, don't you think?

FD: No.

AR: Well, all right. I wanted to ask you about something I've come across in Hughes's diaries, a joke he played on Ava Gardner with a Mercedes.

FD: *(Her face turns wooden.)* Yes, I was baking a cake that day . . . *(She stares at the tabletop.)*

AR: I know what Hughes did to the car. I was more interested in your impressions of the incident.

FD: *(Looking up.)* Yes, well, I guess that day was really the last straw for me. When I saw Howard watching that Mercedes through the binoculars with a big smile on his face, and then saw the muffler come off, well, at that very instant, I knew my days with Howard Hughes were over. I loved him, but at his age, to be pulling stunts like that . . . *(She shakes her head.)* That day I admitted to myself that there was no hope for him.

AR: I see. Okay. Well, can you think of any other incidents, things like this one with the Mercedes, that tell us something about Hughes?

FD: Well, let's see. *(She takes a sip of her coffee.)* I'll tell you, one of my oddest moments with Howard was a day I came home and he—it was a warm spring day, mind you—and he had built a fire in the huge fireplace in our living room. He put down pillows in front of the fireplace and told me to sit down, he needed my help with something. He went down into the basement and came back with these bundles of old letters from his family. He started going through them, reading them aloud before handing them to me to put in the fire. It was so hot next to that fire that I suggested we throw everything in all at once, but he insisted we go on the way we had been. A good number of the letters were from the time after his father died and Howard was trying to get control of his father's tool company. He would read these bitterly and point out how his family betrayed him. [Hughes's father's will was set up so that Hughes would not get full control of Hughes Tool until he was well into his twenties, and until then the company was to be controlled by a group of family trustees. Hughes went to court to get this arrangement changed. At first he was unsuccessful, but then a judge granted him full control of the company after he played a round of golf with him one day—ed.]

AR: Do you remember any specific letters?

FD: *(She considers.)* Just one. It was the only one I tried to convince him to save, a letter his mother wrote from the hospital the day before she died. She was having routine surgery so her death was quite unexpected. Howard started reading this letter aloud but halfway through he stopped. He didn't cry but he handed me the letter and asked me to finish reading it. His mother had beautiful handwriting, and she said tender things to her husband and kind things about Howard. She described how she wanted her belongings distributed if something did happen. She wanted her part of the tool company given to Howard. The pages were blue and the letter was still scented, even after all those years.

After I finished reading Howard said to throw the letter into the fire. I suggested he save it—it was one of his few mementos of his mother—and he looked at me like I was a child who'd just asked why the wind blows. He said the idea we live in the memories of those who survive us is a lie we tell ourselves so we don't go crazy thinking about our own impermanence. He said after we're gone all we are is a name on a rock in a cemetery, and even the famous only had a statue in a park, a different kind of rock. He said the only reason he had saved the letter was in case he had to use it against his relatives in court, and for me to go ahead and throw it in the fire. I didn't, though. I mentioned the filing cabinets down in the basement where he stored everything he wrote, even grocery lists—why not just file the letter down there?—and suddenly he started screaming at me. When had I been down there? I was never to go down there! Well, I started crying. I raised the letter to toss into the fire and then suddenly he said, I've changed my mind, no, no, and he grabbed the letter out of my hand. Then he forced me into an embrace and wouldn't let go until I promised I'd never leave him. I made that promise, but I had serious doubts about being able to keep it. *(She pauses.)* And I guess I was right, because that day with the Mercedes was just a couple of weeks after this.

AR: From everything you're saying, Ms. Domergue, I get the impression you put most of the blame for the failure of the relationship on Hughes.

FD: *(Curtly.)* Who do you think should get the blame?

AR: *(I hold up my hands.)* No offense intended. I was just trying to clarify things.

FD: I was just a girl, Mr. Reece. *(Her mouth is a tight line and she looks away from me.)*

AR: Of course.

(I wait for her to go on, but she doesn't.)

AR: Well, my next question is about a weeklong shopping trip you and Hughes took to Mexico City.

FD: *(She nods.)* We took that trip right after I'd caught him in the car with Ava Gardner one night, in that *same* Mercedes he'd given back to her, right in our own driveway. I let them both know that I didn't— *(The telephone starts ringing. She reaches up for it, hanging on the wall above the table.)* Hello? . . . Yes, this is her . . . Why, my goodness, *how* have you been? It's such a nice surprise to hear from you. Where are you now? . . . Why yes, I'm fine, just going right along . . . Well, yes, what a coincidence. Actually, he's right here . . . *(She stops abruptly, as if interrupted, and listens for at least thirty seconds.)* All right then, I will. Yes, I'll call you in a little bit . . . No, it's here on the caller ID. . . . Thank you for calling. Good-bye. *(She hangs up and then looks across the table at me with a dour expression. I smile and wait for her to speak, but she doesn't.)*

AR: You were saying you found Hughes and Ava Gardner together?

FD: You know, I think we've done enough for today.

AR: *(After a short silence.)* Well, okay, but would it be all right if we set up another appointment? I've got several more questions.

FD: I've probably told you about all I know that's of any interest.

AR: Ms. Domergue, I'd really, *really* appreciate it if we could speak again.

FD: I'm sorry, but I just don't think so.

AR: It sounded like whoever was on the phone knew me. *(A flicker of acknowledgment passes across her eyes, but she doesn't answer.)* Is there some connection between your ending our interview and that call? *(Still no answer. Her face is stony and expressionless.)* Ms. Domergue, I'll have to admit, I'm at a loss here. Did I do something to offend you?

FD: *(Sharply.)* No, I'm just ready to stop. Can't you understand that?

AR: This just seems awfully sudden, Ms. Domergue, and . . . well, if you don't mind me asking, who was that on the telephone?

FD: That's *my* business, young man.

AR: *(Sighing.)* Well, all right. *(I reach for my wallet.)* Here's my card, in case you change your mind. *(I push it across the table and force a smile.)* I'd really like to speak with you again, so I hope you reconsider.

(She doesn't respond, and instead gets up and busies herself at the sink, her back to me. I gather my recorder and other things, and when I'm ready to leave, she escorts me to the front door and says a brief, stiff good-bye. I go out and get in my car, put the key in the ignition, and then glance back at the house. Faith Domergue is standing at the picture window in the living room, watching me, and talking on the telephone again. I sit there a moment, staring at her, then start the car and drive away.)

Alton Reece interview with Ava Gardner at her home in Beverly Hills, California

It's ten o'clock on a bright morning when Ava Gardner's live-in personal assistant, Tom, a well-groomed man in his mid-fifties, ushers me into the high-ceilinged entry foyer of Ms. Gardner's home, asks me to wait, then disappears around the corner—as he leaves his trouser legs rub together and make a noticeable whish-whish. Then there's silence except for a clock ticking loudly in the next room.

A couple of minutes later, Ava Gardner appears, smiling, followed by Tom, and she leads me to a sunporch with a red tile floor and a variety of potted plants along the glass walls. We have a view of the pool and beyond that the orange and lemon trees that ring her backyard. Ms. Gardner and I sit down at a bamboo table; Tom receives his instructions and leaves. Despite her age, seventy-nine, Ava Gardner still has an electric presence. Her skin's pale and surprisingly smooth, her hair's cut short, steel gray with black tints, and she wears baggy black slacks with a thin belt cinching a white blouse at her trim waist.

AR: Ms. Gardner, maybe I'm being presumptuous, but you're as lovely as ever.

AG: Thank you.

AR: What's your secret? I want my wife to have it.

AG: Just lucky, I guess.

AR: You're being modest.

AG: Really, I don't do anything special.

AR: Then you must have made a deal with the devil. That's what I'll have to believe, I guess. *(I smile.)* So, anyway, what can you tell me about Howard Hughes?

AG: Well, since I've known I was going to do this I've been thinking a lot about Howard, and I guess what I can say is outside of a few bad times, he didn't make demands on me and I didn't make demands on him.

AR: No trying to tether each other? No stunting each other's potential?

AG: *(She shrugs.)* I don't know about *that*. Let's just say that when Howard and I did get along, we really got along. If I could've been happily married to any man in my younger days it probably would've been him. Maybe that's why I didn't marry him. In those days, I wanted romance and excitement.

AR: Sure. That nerve never goes numb, does it?

AG: *(A little coolly.)* I really wouldn't know.

AR: All right. Well, did Hughes ever ask you to marry him?

AG: Yes, once he proposed in Palm Springs and handed me two hundred and fifty thousand dollars in a shoe box. I handed it right back and said, "This means nothing to me," and he said, "Me neither." Once he gave me a bag full of jewelry and then waited for my answer. I kept the jewelry for a few days and wore one of the bracelets to a premiere, then gave it all back. I think Howard set up these situations to test me. If I said yes after getting the jewelry or money, then he'd know I was with him for his wealth. That was a great fear of his.

AR: Well, in his situation, I guess it'd be hard to blame him.

AG: *(Smiling sardonically.)* Mr. Reece, do I strike you as a gold digger?

AR: Oh no, I just meant that, generally, when you've got money, you don't always know who to trust.

AG: That was probably right in Howard's case. Take when he died—no one went to the service. It was open, you know, anyone could've gone. I cried when I heard how poorly it was attended. The funeral home was empty. No one but the undertakers were there, so I guess he *was* right not to trust us. (*Then Tom walks in with a tea service and a plate of warm scones. I ask for milk for my tea and he leaves to get it. Then Ava Gardner tries to slice off a pat of butter but the stick is too hard for her to cut through and the knife slips from her hand and clatters loudly on the tray. She looks embarrassed. She picks up the knife again, and, with difficulty, manages to shave off a few slivers of butter and press them onto her scone. Tom returns with a small silver pitcher of milk and sets it on the table.*)

AG: *(Curtly.)* You forgot to set out the butter to soften.

TOM: I'm sorry.

AG: *(She looks across the table at me.)* Don't you think it's too cold to spread? I notice you didn't take any.

AR: It does look pretty hard. *(I smile.)* Ms. Gardner, you know, several times in his diaries Hughes said things to the effect that you were your most charming and attractive when you were in a difficulty of some sort. I can see for myself that's true.

(She nods, embarrassed, but secretly pleased.)

AG: Tom?

TOM: *(Stopping in the doorway.)* Yes?

AG: Please come back and sit down. You might find this interesting.

TOM: Yes, ma'am. *(He comes back and settles into a wicker couch that sits against the glass wall that faces the pool.)*

AR: Well, Ms. Gardner, this is changing the subject, but I wanted to ask you about a story I've come across in one of Hughes's diaries that involved a Mercedes he gave you as a gift and a practical joke he played with it. Do you remember that?

AG: Yes, of course.

AR: When I interviewed Faith Domergue—

AG: *(Interrupting.)* My goodness, is she still out here?

AR: Up in Palo Alto. She's doing fine.

AG: Well good, I'm glad to hear that. *(A pause.)* That Mercedes, yes, of course. I just loved that car. Howard was giving it back to me after I divorced Artie Shaw, and as I drove it away from his house parts just started falling off it. I was so angry! But a few days later Howard had the car delivered to me in pristine condition, completely filled with gardenias. The only thing that really bothered me about the whole thing was that Faith was staring out the window at us the whole time. I have never forgotten how sad she looked. She was just a—*(The doorbell chimes, and she stops a moment.)*—just a young girl then.

(Tom gets up and goes to answer the door.)

AR: Did Hughes ever talk to you about his relationship with Faith?

AG: No. I stayed out of that.

AR: So what was your breakup with Hughes like? What occasioned it?

AG: Well, we had several breakups.

(Tom returns leading three beautiful young women. Two of them look enough alike to be sisters, they're both tall, have dark tans and long brown hair tied back in ponytails; the third girl is shorter, not quite as tan, and has medium-length black hair—she's absolutely stunning, a young Ava Gardner. All three are barefoot, wear shorts and bikini tops, and one of the brown-haired girls has a tiny gold chain around her bare waist. They bring the smell of suntan oil into the room.)

AG: Well look here. What a surprise. *(The girls all say, "Hello, Aunt Ava," and bend down to give her a kiss on the cheek.)*

Mr. Reece, I'd like you meet my grandnieces. This is Alice *(She points to the black-haired girl.)*; Lee *(She points to the girl with the navel chain.)*; and Sarah *(She points to the third girl, who, smiling, dangles a key ring on her finger.)*. Mr. Reece is a writer. He's interviewing me.

AR: Nice to meet you all.

(They all return the greeting.)

AG: The girls are all just starting at UCLA.

ALICE: *(Smiling.)* Well, actually, I'm a sophomore.

AG: Oh, that's right. *(A short pause.)* Mr. Reece, Alice wants to be a writer, just like you are.

AR: *(Smiling at her.)* Is that right?

ALICE: *(She nods.)* I'm planning to major in journalism. *(She pauses, and a look of recognition comes into her eyes.)* Are you the same Alton Reece who did the articles about Madonna in *Rolling Stone?*

AR: Yes.

ALICE: I thought that was a great series. Really interesting.

AR: Thanks.

ALICE: So what was it like following her around?

LEE: *(Cutting in.)* Yeah, does she look as sick in person as she does now on television?

(Alice glares at her, though Lee just smiles back and absent-mindedly twists her navel chain with one finger.)

AR: Yes, well, I thought she looked healthy enough, and, actually, she's quite nice, nothing like the person she's portrayed to be. *(I look back to Alice.)* Would you like to meet her?

ALICE: Yeah, sure. If I could interview her or something that'd be great. I could probably get it in the paper at school.

AR: I can't make any promises, but I'll see what I can do. Her production company bought the film rights to my last book and hired me to write the screenplay, so I have a few dealings with her. *(I take a card out of my wallet, jot my cell number on it, and hand it to Alice.)* Give me a call in a couple of days and I might have some news for you.

ALICE: Thanks.

AR: No problem. I just hope it works out.

AG: I guess you girls are here to swim.

SARAH: *(She swings the key ring around her finger once, making a metallic clack.)* If it's okay with you.

AG: It's always okay. You know that. You don't even have to come in and ask.

(The girls go out through the room's sliding glass door. On the pool apron, they start stepping out of their shorts.)

AR: Lovely girls.

AG: *(She nods.)* Tom, take them something to drink, will you please?

TOM: Yes, ma'am. *(While she finishes giving Tom his instructions, I watch the girls through the glass, their laughter and talking all in mime, their splashes as they jump in the pool just the faintest of whispers.)*

AG: Well, I think we were talking about my breakup with Howard . . . Mr. Reece?

AR: *(I smile.)* Yes, your breakup. Please, go on.

AG: Well, the last time I was ever with Howard we drove down to Palm Springs, and on this deserted stretch of road in the desert we came across a jackrabbit that had been hit by a car. Howard stopped and checked on it and found it was

84

still alive. He got a blanket from the trunk and used it to drag the rabbit out of the road. I was furious. It was hot and we were in one of those old Chevrolets he favored and it had no air-conditioning. I leaned out my window and asked him what the hell he was doing. He was crouched down over the rabbit, and when he looked up I saw tears in his eyes. He said we couldn't just leave it there. I told him he was right and I dug my twenty-two pistol out of my handbag and held it out the window. It had been a gift from Mickey Rooney and was silver with a beautiful pearl handle. I told him to put the poor thing out of its misery but I had forgotten that Howard didn't know I carried a pistol. I'd always managed to keep it from him because I had sensed he wouldn't like it. Howard came to the car and took the pistol. He examined it a long time before he spoke, then asked me if I really wanted him to shoot the rabbit; I said yes, it was in pain, so he'd be doing it a favor. Then he asked me if he was in pain, would I think it was a good idea to shoot him. I didn't let him drag me into all that, though. I just asked him if he was going to kill the rabbit or not. He said if I wanted the rabbit dead, I should shoot it myself. So I unlatched the door and pushed it against his legs until he moved enough for me to get out of the car. I told him to give me the pistol but he raised it above his head, turned his back and fired into the air until it was empty. I said I had more bullets in my purse, but he didn't answer. He put the pistol—*(Then the sliding glass door opens and Ava Gardner and I both look in that direction; Alice is coming back into the room with a yellow towel wrapped around her waist, her black hair slicked down on her head like a helmet. The noise of a radio and the other girls' splashing and banter is audible until Alice closes the door behind her. She approaches our table, leaving a trail of wet footprints and coin-sized puddles behind her on the red tile.)*

AG: Yes, dear?

ALICE: *(She frowns exaggeratedly, playfully.)* I'm bored. I'd like to sit with you and listen in, if that's okay. *(She smiles at me.)*

AG: Well, I suppose that's all right.

AR: Sure.

ALICE: *(She pulls out the table's last empty chair and sits down to my right and Ava Gardner's left.)* Lee and Sarah were driving me crazy, anyway, talking about Madonna.

AG: *(Smiling faintly.)* Do they want to meet her, too?

ALICE: *(Nodding.)* Of course, but they won't admit it.

(Tom appears outside at the pool with a tray that holds glasses, an ice bucket, a two-liter bottle of cola and a pitcher of lemonade.)

ALICE: *(Examining her fingernails.)* So what were you guys talking about?

AG: Howard Hughes. Mr. Reece is writing a book about him.

AR: You were saying he had just fired the pistol into the air . . .

ALICE: *(Her eyes wide.)* A pistol?

AG: It's not as exciting as it sounds, dear. Yes, he fired the pistol until it was empty, then put it in his pants pocket. After that he used the blanket like a hammock to pick up the rabbit and put it in the backseat. We—

ALICE: I'm sorry to interrupt, but what rabbit?

(Ava Gardner recounts the first part of the story to her niece. While she's talking Tom re-enters, whish-whish, and sits down on the wicker couch again.)

AG: So after he got the rabbit in the car we took off again. He absolutely flew down the highway, nearly a hundred miles an hour. I was terrified. I begged him to slow down but he wouldn't. You could hear the rabbit breathing, a kind of rasping. One of its front feet was torn off but Howard had wrapped a handkerchief around the stub. It was on its side and if you leaned over the seat the one eye that was facing up would roll toward you.

ALICE: That sounds awful.

AG: Yes, it was. So Howard stopped at the first gas station we came to and went in and asked if there was a veterinarian in the area. There wasn't, so he called ahead to Palm Springs and arranged for one to be ready when we got into town. I got out of the car with the full intention of not getting back in. I was going to call someone to come out and pick me up. The way Howard was driving . . . *(She shakes her head.)* I wasn't going to risk my own life to save a rabbit's. The men working in the gas station knew who we were. I chatted with them and gave them autographs. A carload of tourists stopped, two young couples, and I took photographs with them. When Howard came back to the car he had a bag of ice and a can of aerosol paint of all things. He told me to get in, we were leaving. I told him I wasn't going another foot with him, not the way he was acting. Do you know what he said? "Suit yourself," and he set my handbag out on the gravel. Then he took the top off the can of aerosol paint and put ice in it and then a squirt of water from the hose at the gas pump. He put the little bowl of water on the blanket for the rabbit. I went over and picked up my handbag and got in the car. *(She pauses, and then smiles.)* If he had tried to convince me to go I wouldn't have. So we went to Palm Springs and he took the rabbit to the veterinarian. Then we got our suite and went to dinner, but during dinner Howard would disappear every half hour or so to call the vet's office and check on the rabbit. It lived and Howard paid that veterinarian to board it until it died, because with one foot missing it never could've survived in the wild again. He supplied the money to have a good size pen built behind the vet's office because he wouldn't allow the rabbit to be put into a cage. I understand he would send a man down there for surprise inspections to make sure the rabbit was being treated well, even in those later years when no one saw him anymore. He would require a photograph of the rabbit be taken and sent to him.

ALICE: He sounds like a great guy.

AG: Yes, what he did for that rabbit was wonderful. But it's hard to stay with a man who just goes off on tangents like that, even if they're good ones.

ALICE: What'd you mean?

AG: Well . . . *(She leans over and picks at something on the heel of one of her white, nurse-looking shoes, then looks up again.)* I think it's somehow connected to the fact that sometimes, well, a lot of women just don't marry the man they really love. You've got too much to lose if you actually love them. I ought to know because I married ones I loved a couple of times and it nearly killed me.

ALICE: So you didn't marry him because you loved him?

AG: No, because I loved him too much.

AR: Ms. Gardner, did you want Hughes to be dull? To . . . I don't know, to just go to a job he hated and then come straight home and putter in the yard until he got called to supper?

ALICE: Yeah, what were you looking for, Aunt Ava? *(After she asks the question our eyes meet briefly and I give her a small nod of encouragement.)*

AG: *(She shrugs.)* I don't know what to tell you. It's very complicated.

AR: Well, I suppose it is. *(I flip pages in my notepad to find my next group of questions, but before I can continue the other two girls open the sliding glass door and come bursting into the room in their bikinis, their wet feet slapping on the tile floor. They plop down on the wicker couch on opposite sides of Tom, who keeps staring ahead blankly.)*

LEE: Mind if we listen too?

AG: Tom, could you please get towels for the girls?

TOM: *(Rising.)* Yes, ma'am.

SARAH: And when you get finished, we'd like to hear all about Madonna.

LEE: *(Laughing.)* That's right, start with the whole dynamic between her and those dancers. There's *got* to be a story there.

AG: Lee, Mr. Reece is working. He doesn't have time for all that.

AR: *(I smile.)* That's okay. I don't mind. *(I turn off the tape recorder.)*

Hughes diary entry from November 3, 1946, continued:

I went inside. Faith was still in the kitchen, only everything was spic and span now, and she was at the table, cleaned up and dressed in a simple yellow dress with a yellow carnation in her hair. She was crying. Her chocolate cake sat alone on the table on a pedestal plate. The cake was three layers but so lopsided it looked like a triangle and the icing was runny and a single cherry sat on top of the cake with the stem sticking up like a hair.

I went up and put my hands on her shoulders and leaned over and kissed the top of her head. Your next one will turn out better I said.

She eased her shoulders away from my hands. It was not a jerk or a pull.

I bet that cake tastes good I said. I've eaten a lot of cakes that didn't look so good but tasted great.

I got a plate, fork and knife and sliced into the cake. She sobbed. I put a bite into my mouth. The icing was grainy and too sweet and the cake itself was bitter and dry. This is delicious I said.

It's not the cake she said.

I put down the fork. Then what is it? Is it because Ava was here? Is it because I talked to Ava?

No.

Then what?

I saw what happened with that car. I saw what you did.

I did that to teach her a lesson. She'll leave us alone from now on.

Don't lie she said. You don't go to all the trouble you did with that car unless you have feelings. You still have feelings for her.

That's not true.

I started to say something else but stopped. Her eyes were puffy and wet. Her makeup was running in black streaks. She looked so beautiful I started crying.

That doesn't move me Howard. How many times have I cried and you continued to go your own way?

I know. I've failed you horribly. You're the only one I can really count on and look what I've done. I don't deserve you. You're only 18 and you're already a better person than I am. I'm 43 years old and I've got no family, no children and no friends. You're all I've got and I've done nothing but hurt you. I've messed up completely.

Outside the Mercedes started. I wouldn't have known if I hadn't seen her head turn in that direction. Down the hill Russelli was a tiny figure standing alongside it and smoke poured from underneath because of the missing tailpipe.

I've heard all this before she said.

I know. I wouldn't blame you if you walked out of this house today and never came back. You being with me as long as you have is better than I deserve. I'm coming clean Faith. I've been seeing other women, yes. I haven't been the man I want to be. But right now, on all I hold sacred, I swear I'm going to change. I'm going to change because of my love for you. I renew my pledge for us to marry.

Who have you been seeing?

I'd rather not get into names. I don't see the point of that.

You're right. I can give them to you just as easily. Ava. Lana. Kathryn. Rita. Jean.

I'm not arguing. I admit it all. Go on.

There's more?

I mean say whatever you want. Tear into me. I deserve it.

The telephone rang. It rang four times and neither of us moved for it. We stared across the table at each other.

You know who that is she said.

Yes and I'm not getting it.

I see. You don't want to talk to her in front of me.

That's not it.

Pick up the phone.

I pushed away from the table and stood up and answered the telephone.

Howard it's me. Can you talk?

It was Lana.

No.

Faith's there?

Yes.

Then call me later.

I hung up and went back to the table and sat down.

Was it her?

Yes. She was screaming. I saw no point in listening to it.

None of this would be happening if you didn't want it to. You could put a stop to all of it.

I know. And I will. Give me one more chance Little Baby. Let me prove my devotion to you.

She stared out the windows. The Mercedes was gone. The sun was setting making everything pale gold.

I'll tell you what I said. I'll get cleaned up and we'll go down to Santa Monica Pier tonight. I'll win you a couple of stuffed bears like I used to. We'll eat cotton candy. It'll be like the old days.

The old days are gone she said.

Don't say that. It breaks my heart to hear you say something like that.

Okay, okay, I'll go.

That's my baby.

In the bathroom I stripped down and turned on the shower. I discarded the old bar of soap using several thicknesses of Kleenex and opened the new bar. I looked at my body in the mirror until it fogged up. Then I got down on my knees at the vanity. I interlocked my fingers and put them on the edge of the vanity and let my head rest on them in the praying position. I closed my eyes but immediately opened them again and stared into the blank surface of the fogged up mirror. I unlocked my fingers and tapped out Morse Code on the vanity marble. *This cake is awful. Help. Faith is a nice girl. I will never pay taxes.* [italics mine] I thought of being a boy in Houston and tapping out messages on a wireless to ships heading to port there. You sent a message out and many times an answer would come back. I thought of those days and my dear mother and father.

I started noticing a peculiar smell. Something so sweet and heavy it was sickening. I scooted back and opened the vanity door and inside were bottles and canisters of lotions and powders and perfumes and makeup and rolled up pairs of silk stockings and a huge tub of cotton balls and brushes full of hair and filthy applicators of various sorts. I shut the cabinet door and staggered to my feet. I felt like I was going to vomit. I sat down on the toilet and picked up the telephone and dialed.

Lana I said.

Howard.

Let's go to Reno tonight. We'll eat dinner there.

Tonight? I don't know.

We have to.

Well all right. Okay, I guess. But Howard, we have to talk. Things can't continue like they have been.

Don't worry, everything's going to change. Definitely. But we need to get out of here. We need to get away.

I said I'd go she said.

I showered, dressed, and when I went downstairs Faith was still in the kitchen.

Sorry Little Baby. I checked in at the plant and they need me there. An emergency with the XF-11 [the experimental reconnaissance plane Hughes was soon to crash—ed.]. I'm sorry. We'll have to go another time. This might take all night.

Okay.

Aren't you upset?

Not really.

Well, that's a nice attitude.

I left and picked up Lana at her place. Fifteen minutes later we were stuck in traffic on Wilshire. She kept asking When are we getting married? When are we setting a date? until finally I said As soon as you shut up which I guess means never.

Damn you she said and made to get out. I reached over and grabbed the door and held it so she couldn't open it and she tore at my arm like a hellcat. Just my luck, that's when traffic started to inch forward again. I didn't move the car right away because she was fighting too hard and I would've wrecked even at a slow speed and I certainly wasn't going to let her get out and then be running after her down Wilshire. She tried to bite my wrist but I jerked my arm away and accidentally clipped her, just lightly, an inconsequential glazing blow in the jaw with my elbow. Traffic was still moving slowly and people behind me started honking their horns. She grabbed her face with both hands and I took my foot off the brake and eased on the gas.

You broke my jaw she screamed.

If your jaw was broken you couldn't talk.

Traffic stopped again.

Goddamit why're you still living with that little bitch? she screamed.

Because you don't just drop someone out of your life all at once, just like that, like they were a suit of clothes you're tired of wearing or a goldfish you're flushing down the toilet. People have emotions and those emotions have to be dealt with. There is a very, very fine line in human relationships, a tricky gray area.

I can't take her being in your house she said. I can't, not one more second.

You know you're the only woman for me. You're all I want. I've never wanted anyone like I want you. I want us to get married and leave all this glamour and glitz behind. You'll still make movies, sure. You'll be an even bigger star than you are now. And I'll get rid of some of the pressures that are absolutely killing me. The pressures are so bad I can barely eat. For the last three days all I've had is pecans and milk. A human being can't live on that forever. I thought if we went to Reno, away from the pressure, all the things that bother us, I could eat. We could have a nice dinner. And when we're married, my mind will be on aviation and nothing but aviation except for you. We'll be together the way a man and woman should be.

Howard do you mean that?

In the eyes of God Lana we're already married.

I want to believe you. I wish I could.

We sat there with the heat coming in the windows and all the horns beeping and the noise of idling engines all around us. Then a goddamn fly came in and started buzzing around.

Well what if I wasn't serious? I am serious, make no mistake about that. I'm dead serious. If you don't marry me I don't know what I'll do. But I'm going to tell you something. I've been hearing stories that could seriously affect my level of seriousness in our situation.

She was rubbing her jaw. I watched her eyes. She knew exactly what I was talking about. I shifted into neutral so I could take my foot off the clutch. Ronald Colman I said.

What?

Don't play innocent with me. I'm not one of these schoolboy dandies you're used to. I'm not so easy to fool.

All right. What if I was seeing Ron? I'm not, mind you. But what if I was? You're living with a 18-year-old for god sakes. And God knows what you do in New York and Miami and wherever else it is you go when you go off.

So it's Ron I said.

Christ she said.

So you are familiar with him, I just want to establish that fact, get it on the table. Ron. Is it okay if I call him Ron too when I say something like fucking Ron is fucking the woman I love and want to spend the rest of my life with. Or should I go ahead and use Ronald in that situation?

What if I did have an innocent evening of some sort with

Ron or anybody else. Wouldn't I have that right? You're living with Faith. What kind of pictures do you think that puts in my head night after night?

What's with this damn traffic? Jesus! I slapped the dash and put the car back in gear. Come on! I said.

Answer me she said. How'd you think that makes me feel?

Look I just explained that situation but if you need to hear it twice, fine. Faith and I are breaking up but it's got to happen slowly so I don't leave her bruised and battered for life. You said it yourself. She's eighteen. She's a girl. I've made a mistake so I have to pay the price of staying with her longer than I want to, when all I want for the rest of my life is to be in your arms. But I'm trying to do the right thing by her. Don't you want your husband to be a guy like that? A decent guy?

She rolled down her window and looked out it awhile at I guess the damn telephone pole sitting there.

Are you going to put her in anything? she said.

What'd you mean?

Give her a part.

When she's ready, yes. That's part of the plan. After I leave her completely and for good and am with you always, she'll get plenty of parts to keep her busy. Her career will replace me. But if you're against it, that's it, I won't do it.

No that's fine. She turned from the window and looked at me, two tears running down her cheeks, one on each side. Fucking actresses. With them tears are a skill, period. But I played along. I smiled. I put my arm around her and asked How's that jaw?

A little sore.

You'll live Gator-gooey.

We were in the old Chevy so we weren't too noticeable but the people in the car next to us on my side, a family, were staring and pointing but I bet they didn't even recognize Lana. Without the high-priced makeup and hair artists she looks about the same as any mildly attractive counter girl.

There had been a wreck up ahead, a large truck had overturned. But we finally made it to Culver City and after landing in Reno I called Faith from the airfield and told her that for certain I would be working all night, the engineers had botched my instructions for the wing stress test beyond all recognition. I told her I would bring her a surprise when I came home. What? she asked. I told her that was the surprise. Then she picked up where she left off about the incident with Ava. She couldn't even shut up for one little supposed call from work. I told her there was nothing I could do about it now. Then she wanted to know how serious I was about renewing my pledge to marry her. Setting a date would prove it to her. I told her whatever date she wanted as long as we waited until fall. Fall was when I'd have my affairs in order, the HK-1 and XF-11 straightened out and on schedule, and then I could give her the attention she deserved.

I don't know why I keep putting myself through this hell. You ask actresses to marry you, you agree to marry them and they feel they have you in their talons like a powerful condor has a titmouse and as soon as that moment of saying yes, I'll marry you happens they drop you, the titmouse, out of their powerful talons and you fall and are crushed but you refuse to marry these actresses and they stay on your back causing more irritation than some kind of goddamn Chinese water torture or a monkey picking constantly at your skin. These women always have to be in the limelight and have the crowds looking at them and oohing and aahing about they are so beautiful or have played such a good part. Actresses look great but they make me sick. Lying is what they do best, except for screwing anyone they think has any kind of decision making power at a studio. That's the number one talent. It would not surprise me one bit to walk in one day and find Ava Gardner screwing the guy who decides what kinds of doughnuts will be on the set for the crew each morning and as they were in the act she'd be looking over the guy's shoulder for the guy who makes decisions about coffee. I'd like to find a decent beautiful nonactress girl and settle down.

For dinner I had steak, mashed potatoes, peas. I forgot to bring my little rake, so I had to separate the too large peas from the correct size ones by hand.

No matter what else is said in the history books a hundred years from now this is the true story of the last day I ever had to be around Ava Gardner or talk to her.

Lana Turner, from a transcript recorded for a UCLA-sponsored oral history of Hollywood's "Golden Age"
Howard Hughes was another one I felt like I just had to marry. I didn't, of course, even though on a trip to Reno one time we set a date and Howard presented me with a diamond I was almost afraid to wear it was so big. But then the morning of the day we're supposed to marry I've already had my hair done and I'm actually putting on my wedding makeup and the telephone rings and it's not Howard, no, it's one of his henchmen telling me the wedding had to be postponed because Howard had to fly

to Washington unexpectedly, he'd been summoned there on a matter of grave national concern. What was it I wanted to know but he wouldn't say. I didn't talk to Howard for weeks after that. I called every day. I called and called and called but Howard was like that, he'd disappear like a dollar bill you just spent.

Make Them Feel Special

After his breakup with Faith Domergue, Hughes was afraid he would never find a woman to settle down with, so, after he bought RKO Studios, he scoured magazines for pictures of beauty-contest winners, festival queens, bit players he found attractive, and then sent aides to sign them up for RKO. He had literally dozens of women under contract. As the following memo indicates, he kept close tabs on all of them, but he also supplied them with beautiful apartments and wardrobes and any kind of appropriate lesson, singing, acting or dancing. He would arrange private screenings of the movies he wanted them to watch for their good as actresses. A few of them won parts in movies, but most didn't. Hughes often had affairs with the women, hoping the relationships would turn into something more, but none of them ever did.

Hughes, from a memo to an aide dated June 19, 1947, and titled "Instructions For Handling Women Under Contract To RKO"

1. When any of our drivers from the Romaine Street office or any of our other locations, Culver City or the office at Goldwyn-Mayer or anyplace else we've set up shop,

permanent or temporary, such as a temporary command post we might set up at an elegant hotel in New York or Miami or Vancouver, these drivers, including Frank, Johnny, any of the crew of Mormons currently employed, or anyone we might employ in the future, when these drivers are transporting our girls under contract from point A to point B, say from the hairdresser to an acting lesson, and they encounter any small obstacle in the road such as a dead animal or a landscaping tool that was poorly secured and fell off the back of a truck, or one of these so-called "speed bumps" that are showing up in parking lots everywhere now, or trash of any sort that might make the vehicle jerk even the most infinitesimal bit, one-thousandth of one-thousandth of an inch, then the driver is to slow the car down to exactly 2 miles per hour—I repeat, no more than 2 miles per hour—so that the girl, sitting in the backseat, will not have to undergo the violent jarring of her breasts and the possible damage to the delicate muscles that support them that going over the obstacle at a higher speed might cause. I want these instructions followed to the letter. I want these drivers monitored in some way. Possibly random tailings of the cars carrying these girls would work—a monitoring system is something you and I need to put our heads together on, Charlie. But we need to do it right away. If the girls ask questions of the drivers such as, Why are we slowing down so often? you are to instruct the drivers to tell them some lie about the nature of automobiles, their suspension systems, or maybe just something about difficulties we're having with the particular car they are in—anything like that should work because most of the girls won't know anything about cars. But under absolutely no circumstances are the girls to be told the car is slowing to protect their breasts. One, I don't want the drivers engaging in conversations with the girls about breasts. The better sort of girl will be embarrassed, the worst sort will see it as an invitation. There is absolutely no reason for the drivers to ever, ever say the word *breasts* [italics mine—ed.] inside these automobiles. Another advantage of this policy is that it precludes the girl arguing with the driver about the policy itself or becoming offended by it and causing trouble in some other way. She might say something about the relative strength of her brassiere or some other such shit and because they are attractive girls, before we know it these goddamned drivers are jumping these cars over obstacles like they're motorcycle daredevils. Forget it. We've got to stick to our guns. Please know, Charlie, that this isn't just some personal quirk I'm indulging. The American public is crazy about breasts. You know it and I know it. Look at our success with Jane Russell and *The Outlaw* [italics mine—ed.] and I think you'll see why this policy has to be implemented right now, today, as soon as you finish reading this memo. If we ever expect to have even the slightest hope of getting a return out of our investment in these girls, and getting this studio out of the god awful morass it's in right now, which would certainly help with all the other financial woes that are plaguing us right now, you'll implement this policy with all due haste.

2. For the same reason stated in point one, the girls, whenever possible, are to be prevented from diving off diving boards or platforms of any sort and under absolutely no circumstances are they to be allowed to jump off the sides of boats of any kind. Maybe they are at a Sunday sailing party and they have a few drinks. This is acceptable. But then the boat anchors and they want to jump off the side of the boat into the water to swim and roughhouse with the other guests. This is not acceptable. At this point, if you see such a situation developing, you are to find a quick excuse and whisk the girl away from the side of the boat.

3. The girls are to be discouraged from eating ice cream. However, if they insist, they are to have no more than one ice cream cone a day. That is the absolute, final limit. If they want more, tell them stories about young actresses we've had under contract who didn't make the grade because of excess weight. If they ask for names, tell them you don't remember and that fact itself demonstrates the extent of their failure. However, once the Rubicon has been crossed and the girl is determined to have ice cream, push french vanilla as the flavor of choice. It does the least damage.

4. No pork. If they want meat with breakfast, suggest a minute steak. If they want a pork chop for dinner, suggest lamb. If that doesn't work, start raising hell about something else. And they should never even be in the vicinity of a plate, fork, knife, or spoon that has ever been touched by a hot dog or any of this canned bulk sausage.

5. If any of these girls get impatient for a meeting with Mr. Hughes, tell them Mr. Hughes is impatient for a meeting with them, too, you heard him talk about it just the other day, but that vital government work—something about the H-bomb and the Communists, something like that, something that's on everybody's mind and in the news and that throws Mr. Hughes in the best possible light—is keeping him tied up.

6. To whatever extent humanly possible, make sure that as few girls as possible know about the existence of other girls like themselves, under contract to us and receiving the same grooming. Make them feel special.

Marriage

On January 12, 1957, Howard Hughes ended the long romantic journey we've witnessed so far by marrying actress Jean Peters in a secret ceremony at Tonopah, Nevada, which was now— almost thirty years after his visit there with Billie Dove—a half-deserted silver-mining town in an area used for underground atomic testing; on January 6, he had begged actress Kathryn Grayson to marry him and had been refused; and a week before that, on New Year's Eve, 1956, he carried out the elaborate plans dictated in the following memo.

Hughes memo to Chanson O'Reilly, Hughes's head of security from 1951 to 1971. The memo is dated December 3, 1956, and titled "New Year's Eve Plans"

1. Miss Peters will be seated in the main dining room. At

her table will be violets and the German wine that is her favorite. Miss Hayward will be at the top notch table in the Polo Lounge, no champagne, and when our man seats her he is to present her with gardenias and the ruby ring you obtained last week for this purpose. Miss Schubert will be in a bungalow in the tropical garden section of the grounds. She's to have Dom Perignon and yellow roses.

2. The order of accompaniment will be Peters, Hayward, Schubert. I will spend fifteen to twenty minutes with each woman, then one of our men will rush in with an urgent matter that requires my attention. I will make apologies, kiss the date, then rush away. This cycle will repeat itself until the evening is finished.

3. When the evening is finished, each woman will expect to be with me. I haven't decided who I'm going to be with or how I'm going to escape from the other two. There'll be a memo on this subject later.

4. This operation will require twenty men stationed at various points throughout the hotel and its grounds. Their duty will be to intercept any woman who strays from her area toward a danger zone where I am engaged with a different woman. Thursday we will determine the best places to station the men.

5. Following is the list of excuses to be used by the men assigned to call me away from the tables. Make sure each man has a carbon of these. They must be used in the order they appear.

    a) There's been a fire of some sort at the tool company, Mr. Hughes. Houston's on the phone.

b) You have another call from Houston, Mr. Hughes. Your lawyers. Something about the fire.

c) Vice President Nixon's on the phone, Mr. Hughes. He sounds intoxicated and says he won't stop calling unless you come speak to him.

d) I'm very sorry to bother you again, Mr. Hughes and Miss_____. Happy New Year to you both. Mr. Hughes, it's Vice President Nixon again. He's called three times since you talked to him. We don't know what to do.

e) Please excuse me again, Mr. Hughes, but one of your lawyers working on the TWA situation is on the phone from New York. Goodness, who works on New Year's Eve? Anyway, he would like to speak to you.

f) This is amazing. This is a New Year's Eve for the books. But Mr. Hughes, Mr. Dietrich is on the telephone from Houston. Something else about this gosh darn fire.

Alton Reece interview with Chanson O'Reilly at his daughter's home in San Diego, California

I meet Chanson O'Reilly at a tract house of the type being built nowadays that looks like it's about half garage; his daughter Rella, a small, pretty woman with short red hair and freckles, answers the door. After we exchange greetings, she tells me she read Melville and the Whale *and enjoyed it a great deal. I thank her. She leads me down a hallway to a closed door, and, with her hand on the doorknob, whispers an apology about her father's bedroom being so warm—he has poor circulation. We enter. Chanson O'Reilly sits in a brown vinyl recliner beside a four-poster bed, a patterned afghan over his legs. The folding television tray next to his chair is crowded with pill bottles, a box of tissues, a can of Ensure with a flexible straw sticking up out of it. I sit down in a straightback chair at the foot of the recliner. Rella asks if I'd like anything to drink and I say some water would be nice, then she asks if it's all right if she sits in on the interview and I say certainly. After she leaves to get my water a boy of five or six wearing a Michael Jordan jersey enters and runs up to the recliner, leans against the armrest and stares shyly at me.*

CO: This is my grandson Neil.

AR: Hello there, Neil.

(He looks at the floor.)

CO: How old are your children, Mr. Reece?

(Before I can answer Rella enters and hands me a glass of sparkling water with a lime wedge, then sits down on the edge of the bed. I take a sip, then set the glass at my feet.)

AR: Actually, Mr. O'Reilly, my wife and I are waiting to start a family.

RELLA: A lot of people do that nowadays.

CO: No, family isn't as important to people as it used to be. *(He shakes his head.)* All these women having babies without getting married.

RELLA: *(Smiling stiffly.)* Dad, please.

AR: Do you think things have changed for the worse, Mr. O'Reilly?

CO: Yep.

AR: I do, too, mostly because we don't have heroes anymore who're worth a dime. We're just a peacock culture—whoever's flashiest or loudest gets the attention. Just look at sports, if you don't believe me. There's no one today even close to being the kind of hero Howard Hughes was.

CO: *(He scoffs.)* Howard Hughes wasn't a hero.

(There's a short silence. Rella smiles at me apologetically.)

NEIL: Michael Jordan's good.

RELLA: Of course he is, honey.

CO: *(Reaching over to pat Rella's knee.)* You know, why don't you and Neil let us talk by ourselves?

RELLA: Well, all right, I guess, if that's what you want. *(She stands up.)* Come on, Neil. *(Smiling.)* Mr. Reece, I'll see you before you leave.

AR: Certainly. *(They leave the room and she shuts the door behind them.)* Well, okay, Mr. O'Reilly, the first thing I wanted to ask you about were the New Year's Eve plans Hughes made in 1956, the ones involving having dinner with three women at the same time.

(He nods, reaches for a tissue and wipes some saliva from the corner of his mouth, then picks up the remote, turns on the television sitting behind me, and switches channels until he finds The Price Is Right.*)*

CO: I like having this on.

AR: *(I hide my irritation by smiling.)* Fine with me. So, could you tell me what happened that night?

CO: *(Gazing past me at the screen.)* Nothing unusual. He just treated some women like hell.

AR: Do you remember any of the specifics?

CO: Son of a bitch would call me at home in the middle of

the night every time he had some new idea about planning it—I sure remember *that. (He gives a disgusted wave.)* He had diagrams, timetables, men with walkie-talkies—goddamned place looked like the goddamned president was visiting.

AR: I know things didn't work out as planned.

CO: *(Nodding.)* He blamed me.

AR: So what happened?

CO: He made one round of the women okay, but by the second time he left Miss Peters she was looking around, fidgeting— she knew something was wrong. She got up to look for him and I tried to stop her, but she found him with Miss Hayward in the Polo Lounge. *(He smiles.)* They both walked out on him.

AR: And the other woman? Yvonne Schubert?

CO: That's where he spent the night, the son of a bitch.

(Outside in the street, an ice-cream truck playing a loud, tinny version of "La Cucaracha" stops; I hear it first, then see it through the window.)

CO: You know, she was eighteen and he was *fifty-two,* for chrissakes. *(He leans forward in the chair and shakily props himself with one hand on the armrest. He points a finger at me.)* I want you to have a clear picture of this son of a bitch. He *always* had a lot of women, not just this one night. There were whores, coeds, actresses, dancers, clerks, nurses, one right after the other. He was like a rat on a goddamned wheel.

AR: *(Smiling, trying to lighten the mood.)* I guess if you've got to be a rat, that's not a bad wheel to be stuck on.

CO: But some of them weren't adults! *(He makes a fist and bangs it down on the recliner's armrest.)* Some of them were just girls! You . . . he . . . *(He's too angry for words; his face is florid.)* Did you know . . . *(He sputters.)* These women, their apartments were bugged. Their telephones were tapped. We watched them constantly. *(He taps a finger violently against his sunken chest.)* I arranged it. It was my job. I was making three times what I could've . . . *(He pauses, and when he speaks again his voice is low.)* I wanted to be a police officer, but that's what I did instead. *(He stares blankly at his feet at the end of the footrest. Then, sounding faraway and distracted.)* I drilled a peephole into Miss Schubert's bedroom.

AR: That night at the hotel?

CO: No, no, at her apartment. Hughes had me do it. He wanted to make sure no other man was ever in there except him. But my men started watching her and Hughes have at it. I ended up with five or six in there watching. *(He looks at me with a helpless expression.)* I couldn't fire them. They had families.

AR: That's a difficult situation. *(I pause.)* Mr. O'Reilly, would you excuse me a moment? I need to stop for a moment. I'm going to step out into the hallway here, if that's okay.

Alton Reece cell phone call to Tom Lourdes, during a break in interview with Chanson O'Reilly:

AR: Tom, hi, Alton Reece. Hey, I came across some things about Jean Peters in your notes that I wanted to ask you about. You had some comments about Hughes's New Year's Eve dinner plans in 1956, when he tried to have dinner with three women at once and Jean Peters was one of them. The word *begging* was next to Jean Peters's name . . .

TL: *(After a pause.)* Benny.

AR: Who's Benny?

TL: A waiter at the hotel.

AR: A source?

TL: Yes. He said Jean Peters was crying. He said she stood at his table and cried and then she said one word, *why*, and nothing else. The other actress slapped him.

AR: That'd be Susan Hayward. *(I wait, but he doesn't respond. Through the door I hear the volume on Mr. O'Reilly's television grow louder.)* Well, do you know anything about Yvonne Schubert? I'm talking to a former Hughes head of security who says Hughes had a peephole drilled into her bedroom. People were watching her and Hughes have sex. *(He still doesn't respond. I can hear his raspy breathing.)* Okay, he also says Hughes slept with literally hundreds of women, that he had an insatiable sexual appetite. Anything to say yea or nay on that? I'm trying to find an angle to take on this interview. I'd really appreciate—

TL: *(Interrupting.)* Look, young man, if you see Hughes as some kind of s-s . . . *(He can't finish the word.)* sexual . . . Superman, you're wrong. He wasn't even Clark Kent. He was a Jimmy. And that's all I've got to say. *(He hangs up.)*

Hughes memo to Chanson O'Reilly, titled "Mr. Hughes's Wedding Plans" and dated January 9, 1957

1. Have a Constellation fueled up and ready at the Culver City field by 7 a.m. Tuesday morning.

2. I will fly the airplane.

3. We will go to Tonopah, Nevada—this should lose the press vultures hovering over us constantly right now. Who

would suspect such a godforsaken place as the sight [*sic*] for my wedding? There are two hotels in Tonopah. Determine which is the classiest and rent two floors of rooms. This will be our staging area. Make arrangements to have the lobby clear and secure between 10 a.m. and 2 p.m. and have the town's justice of the peace waiting. The man who makes these arrangements can also secure the wedding license. On the license I will be called G. A. Johnson and Jean will be called Marian Evans.

4. On the morning of the 12th, I will unexpectedly call two colleagues at exactly 5 a.m. and tell them I need them to accompany me on a journey of the utmost importance. All of us, Jean included, will dress as duck hunters. To add to the duck hunter disguise, the men will not shave. I will sneak out of the house before dawn and walk to 10th Street. Pick me up in front of the butcher's shop there. We will appear to be two pals going off on a hunting expedition. This should trick the scavenging, shit-eating birds.

5. There will be no loading stairs to accommodate a Constellation at the Tonopah airstrip, so bring a good length of rope for exiting and re-entering the airplane.

6. As soon as the ceremony is finished, we will return to Los Angeles. Jean will not be able to climb the rope to re-enter the airplane so you and the other men will go up first, then pull her up into the airplane as she clings to the rope and I remain on the ground to catch her in case she falls.

7. The ring for Jean will be our best red ruby, you know the

one. Get it out of storage at the Romaine Street office and also go to a jewelry store and buy a simple gold wedding band for me, not the cheapest but not the most expensive. You can get my finger size at Romaine Street. I would tell you but damned if I can't find a cloth tape measure.

Alton Reece interview with Chanson O'Reilly, continued:

AR: Mr. O'Reilly, I just spoke with a source on my cell phone and he mentioned a waiter at the Beverly Hills Hotel named Benny.

CO: *(Staring at the television, nodding.)* Everyone knew Benny.

AR: Was he reliable?

CO: No. He'd make up stories to get paid.

AR: Did Susan Hayward slap Hughes that New Year's Eve night, and was Jean Peters crying?

CO: Who said that?

AR: Tom Lourdes, a reporter back then. He said this Benny told him that.

CO: *(He nods.)* I remember Lourdes. No, Hughes didn't get slapped and Jean Peters wasn't crying.

AR: *(After a pause.)* Did Hughes actually know Tom Lourdes?

CO: Kind of, yeah. He mentioned him sometimes. They weren't buddies or anything, but Lourdes was about the only reporter whose guts he didn't hate.

AR: All right. Well, I wanted to ask you about Hughes's wedding to Jean Peters.

CO: Huh. If hell has a circus it won't look much different than that wedding. *(He shakes his head.)* All of us were dressed like duck hunters, except Miss Peters. I wish I had a picture. It looked like the end of a Bob Hope movie.

AR: How'd you keep the press from getting wind of the marriage?

CO: I made all the arrangements myself.

AR: Did Hughes and Jean Peters act like newlyweds?

CO: Yeah, on the way back they sat up in the cockpit and held hands. She'd put her chin on his shoulder and whisper in his ear and he'd nod like he understood, but I doubt it. By that time he could barely hear anything.

(I thank Chanson O'Reilly for his help, leave his room, and go find Rella in the kitchen. Lunch is on the table: cold melon soup, turkey-and-mushroom wraps, spinach salad with hot bacon vinaigrette. A copy of Melville and the Whale *is next to one plate. She asks if I'll sign it and also offers lunch. Despite the fact staying will make me late for an appointment at the Hughes Archives, I sit down. She takes a tray to her father, and while she's gone I sign the book. Then I set up my recorder and turn it on.)*

RELLA: *(Smiling.)* Okay, let's see what you wrote. *(She reads.)* Mr. Reece, you're too kind.

AR: Everything I said is true.

RELLA: Thank you. Well, dig in.

AR: It looks great. *(We both start on our soup.)* This is delicious.

RELLA: Thanks. *(She pauses.)* Mr. Reece?

AR: Yes?

RELLA: Why is your tape recorder running?

AR: *(I put down my soup spoon and she follows suit and looks at me attentively.)* I thought you might be able to give me a different angle on your father's years working for Hughes. Since you wanted to sit in on your father's interview.

RELLA: I'd love to help, but I guess I don't know much. *(She picks up her spoon again.)* You know, I'm curious, though. Why did he want me to leave? What was it he didn't he want me to hear?

AR: Probably the sex stuff.

RELLA: *(She smiles.)* He's so old-fashioned.

AR: Well, he's part of his generation. He can't help that. *(We continue eating. The melon soup is thick, cool, and tart.)* So is there *anything* you can think of from those years when your father worked for Hughes?

RELLA: Well, let me think. *(She stares at the tabletop, then her face lights up and she reaches over and touches my arm.)* I do remember something. Velma, my second oldest sister, she was a teenager in the early sixties, and I was just little, you know, six or seven—

AR: I think you're lying.

RELLA: What?

AR: I don't believe you're that old.

RELLA: *(Blushing.)* Now you're kidding me.

AR: *(Smiling.)* No, but sorry I interrupted. Please, go on.

RELLA: I haven't thought about this in years, but I remember a big argument Velma had with Dad. I think Howard Hughes had somehow seen Velma, and she *was* a beautiful girl. On Friday night there'd be more boys on our front porch than there were at the pool hall. I was always a little jealous of her.

AR: You've got no reason to be.

RELLA: Thank you. *(She touches my hand.)* Now, I might have this all mixed up, but I think Howard Hughes wanted to train Velma to be an actress. He wanted to sign her to a contract at his studio. Velma was all for it and my mother was too, but Dad put his foot down. He said Velma shouldn't have such unrealistic dreams. She and Mom both said what was wrong with at least trying? The contract would've been for a lot of money too. But Dad wouldn't hear it. Velma was seventeen then and Dad would've had to sign for her but he said he'd die first. As soon as Velma turned eighteen she contacted the people at Hughes's studio, but they weren't interested anymore. It always seemed weird to me that Dad wouldn't at least let her try. I mean, he worked for Hughes himself. Did he say anything about that?

AR: No, he didn't mention your sister, but I think he has some resentments about Hughes that color the way he sees him. But that's understandable. He's got the natural resentment of employee for employer. That's always a skewed relationship anyway, even when it's good. Work for someone long enough and you end up thinking he's the devil himself.

Hughes diary entry, January 12, 1957
I married Jean today. She is a wonderful girl and I hope to make her happy.

However, I do not have a good record in this department.

*Alton Reece interview with Jean Peters at her apartment in the
Molvado Retirement Village in Houston, Texas*

*I arrive at Jean Peters's gated community around lunchtime; the
uniformed guard, a young black man with a British accent, asks
my name and business, then disappears into his hut; the city is
under the threat of a hurricane warning and maybe because of this
the cloudless, bright blue sky seems eerie and menacing. The guard
reappears and says that according to his information I'm supposed to
be in a black Lexus with California license plate CXE 113, not a
station wagon, so he'll need to see my driver's license. I hand it over
and he examines it, then hands it back and apologizes for the mix-up.
Then he pauses, as if listening to something, and says from the way my
engine's whistling it sounds like I might have a valve problem. He once
had an old Ford station wagon just like mine, he says, and it gave him
all kinds of problems. I thank him, say I'll have it checked out, and
then he gives me directions and opens the gate; as I make the winding
drive I'm nervous—I feel that in Jean Peters's presence I'll be closer
to Hughes than I have been before: this is the woman who understood
him well enough to marry him. I make a wrong turn—the complex is
huge—and drive another five minutes through the immaculate streets,
neatly landscaped in the medians with dwarf trees and fiery red bushes,
before I somehow arrive at Jean Peters's ground-floor apartment. After
I ring the bell, a good two or three minutes passes before she answers,
and when she does she's leaning on a black cane, a polite smile on her
face. She explains she recently fell going down some steps and twisted
her knee, and motions me ahead of her down a hallway that leads to
the breakfast nook, where I go and then stand and watch her hobble
toward me, her eyes watching the floor ahead of her. She still possesses*

117

the same understated beauty she did in her youth. Her hair is silver now, and her face wrinkled, but in her these seem less signs of decay than of wisdom, when taken together with the indefinable quality—a depth, a peace, a beautiful resignation—that emanates from her blue eyes.

She leans against a counter lined by three tall black leather stools and asks me if I want anything to drink. I say I'm fine, and then she makes her way to the table, sits down, and motions for me to do the same. Two windows are next to the table, and as I'm setting up my tape recorder she asks if the sun bothers me. I say it's in my eyes just a little, and she leans over and twists the rod on the blinds.

AR: Mrs. Peters, you stipulated this interview had to be recorded word for word in the book and I want you to know I completely understand your concerns about accuracy. *(I smile.)* Let me start out by saying I'm quite honored to have the opportunity to speak with you about Howard Hughes. I know you've always refused requests for interviews about him. Why is that?

JP: For one, a person's private life should be private, and, well, the press, reporters, what's called the media nowadays, all helped to kill Howard, in my opinion. They hounded him. Since his death they've also destroyed his memory, made a joke out of him. I never wanted to participate in that.

AR: Well, I hope you know I'm writing a book unlike all the others about Hughes. And I'm not part of the media, either, I'm not a journalist, no journalist would do the kind of book I did on Herman Melville. I have a different way of telling a story and I think it'll work well for Howard Hughes. In fact—and I hope this eases any fears you might have about talking to me—as I've learned more about Hughes I've come to feel a real kinship with him. As a matter of fact . . . *(I pause.)* You know, hold on just a second. I think you might enjoy seeing this. *(I reach under the table and open my blocky pebbled leather case and pull out the brown fedora Hughes wore when he made his test flight of the "Spruce Goose" in 1947. As I punch out the dents in the hat she watches me with interest. I set the hat on the table between us.)* This was his.

JP: Well, isn't this something? *(She reaches out and touches the hat on its brim.)* The only place I know of that would have something like this is the Hughes Archives. I've asked them for a few things and haven't gotten anywhere. They said nothing could leave the premises.

AR: You'd think of all people they'd honor your requests. That place . . . *(I shake my head.)* It's a glorified humidor, and the people running it are on a power trip. I don't know why, but every time—*(My cell phone starts ringing.)* Oh, I'm sorry. I forgot to turn this thing off. The voice mail will pick up. *(We wait, but the phone keeps ringing; I smile embarrassedly.)* Only two people use this number much, my editor and my wife, so I know who to call back.

JP: Maybe you should get it.

AR: Well, maybe I better. Looks like I left the voice mail off, and also like they're not giving up. Excuse me just a moment. *(I flip open the phone.)* Hello? . . . I can't right now . . . Look, Alene . . . This doesn't have to become a legal situation unless . . . Look, I've got to go, I'm in the middle . . . At eight . . . *(I turn off the phone and close it.)* I'm sorry. That won't happen again. Well, I suppose we should get started talking about Hughes, shouldn't we? *(She smiles and nods.)* Are you comfortable describing how you two met?

JP: Certainly. William Hearst was giving a weekend yacht party and Audie Murphy and I went to it together, and Howard was there. He started tagging along wherever we went, then asked us if we'd like to go up in his seaplane. Howard arranged it so I sat up front with him and Audie sat behind us. Up in the air Howard did aerial tricks, rolls, things like that. Then after the party, he just started calling me. *(Her face lights up.)* I loved talking to him, he was so intelligent and funny, and eventually we started dating. We'd go together for a while, but then I'd find out about one of his other women and I'd break up with him. He'd make promises and I'd take him back. That went on for years. I had to keep—*(Her telephone starts ringing. Because of her injured knee, she asks if I could bring her the handset, which she thinks is in the living room. I hurry in there and look around but don't see it; then I notice a silver hairpin with a pearl head on the carpet near the coffee table. I pick it up, examine it, and put it on the coffee table. The ringing stops, and Jean Peters calls out and asks me to look for the phone in the laundry room, which is just off the entry foyer. In there, I find the handset on the dryer; the caller ID screen says Horton Landry called, a Houston number. On the shelving there's a box of All detergent, a bag of bird seed, a grass-stained pair of white Keds, a stack of old newspapers. I take the handset back to the breakfast nook and sit down. She examines the caller ID.)* I need to return this. It won't take a moment. *(She dials. I stare out the narrow gap between the edge of the blinds and the window frame. The sky has darkened some and the wind has picked up enough that tree branches are swaying.)* Hello, H.

L., it's me . . . I'm fine . . . No, we're still talking. We've just started really . . . Well, an hour, let's say . . . Yes . . . Yes . . . All right, see you then. *(She puts the handset on the table.)* A gentleman friend of mine is coming over. We're going to drive inland to ride out this hurricane at his son's home. *(I nod.)* Let's see, I was talking about dating Howard . . .

AR: Yes, and if I'm not mistaken, didn't you marry someone else during those years?

JP: Yes, I left Hollywood and moved to Washington, D.C., with my new husband, but after two months Howard called my husband and told him to ask me whether I still loved Howard Hughes or not. Randall did that, and as much as I wanted to, I couldn't lie. So I went back to Howard. I got my marriage annulled.

AR: Did Hughes change his behavior?

JP: No, he kept playing around.

AR: Why did you put up with it?

JP: I thought that somehow things would work out. Years later, after he got so bad, so ill, I did leave. I had to. When I divorced Howard I hadn't actually seen him for three years. But even then it was hard.

AR: Why?

JP: I loved him.

AR: Yes, of course. All right, the next question I have is about your wedding. Would you care to talk about that? I know the details of it.

JP: *(Smiling.)* Well, then you know it was different. I wouldn't have planned things that way. But still, all in all, I'd say it was the happiest day of my life. *(She reaches for the cord on the blinds and fiddles with it absentmindedly.)* Amazing, isn't it?

AR: I think that kind of loyalty and depth of feeling is quite admirable. There are plenty of wives who can't even accept little inconveniences like their husband's career requiring travel.

JP: Oh, I know what a fool I was for putting up with Howard. I would never advise anyone else to do it.

AR: But you also said your marriage was the happiest day of your life.

JP: Yes, I loved Howard and I couldn't help that, I was happy for that love, but it also nearly killed me. *(At this point on the tape, the wind outside is audible.)* Goodness, listen to that.

AR: Do you consider the problems in the relationship Hughes's fault?

JP: Well, I was a big girl. I did what I wanted to. I was with him because I wanted to be.

AR: That's really refreshing. I've talked to Faith Domergue and Ava Gardner and they both seem to blame Hughes for everything.

JP: Well, I'm not saying Howard wasn't mostly to blame.

AR: God, I'm so tired of hearing that.

JP: Excuse me?

(I reach over and turn the tape recorder off. My arm brushes against her cane, hooked over the edge of the table, and it clatters to the floor. I apologize, retrieve the cane and lean it against the table again. Then she reminds me of our original agreement and says we won't continue unless I turn the recorder back on.)

AR: I'm sorry I said that. It had nothing to do with you. It's just that sometimes I feel like . . . I feel like Hughes is being crucified. I can understand a lot of what he went through since I moved to Beverly Hills myself. The pressures, the temptations, it's all there in that town, in your face every day. *(I pause.)* Don't get me wrong, though, I love it out there. I feel like I was wasting my life before I moved there.

JP: I'll have to admit I hated Beverly Hills.

AR: You know, my wife did too. She stayed a few weeks, then moved back to Baltimore. Like it or not, though, I had to stay.

JP: Really? I'd think a writer could work anywhere.

AR: Yes, that's true, but I'd just paid a *lot* of money for a house and I couldn't afford to turn right around and put it back on the market and maybe sell at a loss, and I also needed to stay out there and get myself established with the right people while my book about Melville was still hot. I went to parties, meetings, made all the rounds—I'm sure you know the drill. My wife, God bless her, just didn't understand. She's a wonderful woman, but she doesn't have a head for business.

JP: Your Melville book was optioned, wasn't it?

AR: Yes, and this one too. I'm doing the screenplays for both of them.

JP: Who's got the rights?

AR: A new production group called Isis has already bought the rights to this one, and Madonna's production company took *Melville.*

JP: *(Smiling.)* Madonna? She and Melville seem an odd couple.

AR: Well, she liked these *Rolling Stone* articles I did on her, et cetera, et cetera—you know how it works. One thing led to another. The way things are going, though, if *Melville* ever gets made they're going to shoot it in black-and-white and jiggle the camera every other shot and think they've done something.

JP: That's just the movie business. You'll get used to it.

AR: I'm sure I will. That's what one of my assistants said, too. She said I was moving into a new phase of my life. She said my "soul was adjusting to a new reality." Of course, she's been graduated from college all of two years. *(I shake my head and smile.)* I've got two other assistants about the same age and they're all at each other's throats. They call me at all hours. *(I pause.)* We've gotten a little off track, haven't we? We're not going to have to include this last exchange in your interview, are we? And since I'm thinking about it, the phone calls, really, what would be the use of keeping those?

JP: Alton, you mentioned the kinds of things that might happen to your screenplay?

(I nod.)

JP: Well, I spent my whole life having that happen to my work. Directors and film editors would cut and paste and misrepresent, and I'm tired of it.

AR: Please reconsider. You'd have full approval over any edits.

JP: *(She shakes her head.)* There are just too many things that could go wrong. I've had that arrangement before, but when the story appeared it was different than what I approved and once something's published the damage is done. And this is too important to me. I've got to make sure the truth about Howard is told.

AR: I see. Well, I guess it doesn't make any difference. Not now.

JP: What'd you mean?

AR: Nothing. I'm just talking. *(I smile.)* Well, okay. I wanted to ask you about the time right after you and Hughes married, when he disappeared and went into seclusion in a screening room.

JP: Yes, that was an awful time. I didn't know where he was exactly . . . *(She pauses. Her expression looks troubled.)* You know, Alton, before we go on, there's something I need to tell you. This has been bothering me since we started, and I like to be completely honest, so I'm just going to do that. Do you know Tom Lourdes?

AR: Yes?

JP: Well, he called me and advised against talking to you, and if I did, he advised that I insist on having full editorial control. I'm telling you because I don't want you to find it out later, and think *that's* why I insisted you use all my interview. I'm doing that for my *own* reasons, I want you to understand that. It has nothing to do with Tom Lourdes.

AR: I see. What exactly did he say?

JP: He said he didn't think you had the proper attitude toward Howard.

AR: Good Lord. *(I sigh, and then for roughly ten seconds there's silence on the tape, except for the faint sound of the wind howling outside. I stare at the floor, my forehead propped between the thumb and forefinger of one hand.)*

AR: *(Looking up.)* You don't agree with him, do you?

JP: Well, I didn't know what to think, but since we've been talking, I've seen that—

(Suddenly hurricane sirens sound, loud, high-pitched, continuous.)

JP: Oh my goodness.

AR: What does that mean?

JP: It means it's close. Now, Alton, about Tom Lourdes. I knew him when I was working as an actress and he's basically a decent man. I'm sure you two can work out whatever differences you have. *(The doorbell rings.)* Oh, that'll be H. L. He must've decided to come early. Could you please let him in for me? I'd appreciate it. *(I go answer the door, and exchange greetings with H. L. Landry, a trim, reserved, handsome man of around seventy, with short gray hair and a neat gray moustache—he immediately calls to mind an English aristocrat, except for his slow Texas accent. We walk back to the breakfast nook.)*

JP: I guess you two met. *(We say yes.)* Well, H. L., I suppose we should go. My bag's packed in the bedroom, if you could get it.

HL: Certainly, dear.

JP: Alton, have you got a safe place to stay for the hurricane?

AR: Yes, I'll be fine. *(I start gathering my papers and putting them in my case.)*

JP: Where are you?

AR: *(I chuckle.)* On the fifteenth floor of the Sheraton. Three blocks from the shore.

JP: Oh my goodness.

AR: I'm sure I'll be all right. *(After my hurried, haphazard packing, there's not room in the case for Hughes's fedora, so I carry it in my free hand.)* Thank you again, Mrs. Peters. I can't tell you how much I appreciate you talking to me.

JP: Yes, of course. *(She reaches up and pats me on the arm.)* And you be careful. If it gets bad, get out of that hotel.

ODYSSEY

I T TAKES COURAGE to go on an odyssey, and Howard Hughes did it not just once, but several times. However, he doesn't end up like Ulysses, that most famous of travelers, home again, happy, maybe just a little discomfited by domestic tedium; no, Hughes's odysseys describe an unfolding tragedy. On the surface his adventures seem just like those of Ulysses: outlandish, improbable, quixotic. The difference between them, though, and it's an important one, is that all of Hughes's adventures are true. They actually happened. The suffering is real, and there's no happy literary ending. In fact, what strains our credulity when we hear these stories about Hughes is that no matter how fantastic they are, we know they actually happened. We must remember, though, that Hughes had a lot of money and very little concern for social convention and this combination gave him the capacity to do whatever he wanted.

In this section, we first see Hughes not long after Billie Dove left him. After a disturbing incident in a barbershop in Beverly Hills, he goes to Fort Worth, takes on a false identity to get a job with American Airlines, and establishes a relationship with a young woman, Janice Trundle. We next see Hughes ten years later, not long after he's crashed a plane into Lake Mead in Nevada. As soon as the plane is recovered, Hughes takes off in it with two mechanics (Russelli and Tompkins from "A

Gift Is A Gift") on a rambling eighteen-month journey and everywhere he goes he takes along a large box, which I'll say more about later. In this episode Hughes is really starting to lose touch, the tragedy is accelerating, and this continues when he is under subpoena from the Senate on charges of war racketeering and avoids federal marshals by hiding out and paying someone else to go on his odyssey for him, a man named Brucks Randall, an out-of-work actor who is a dead ringer for Hughes and travels around impersonating him. Hughes gives Randall lists of instructions to carry out that have nothing to do with avoiding the marshals, and these lists (read them as Lear raging on the heath or Hamlet muttering in the palace) reveal Hughes's belief he is a complete failure. Finally, not long after his marriage to Jean Peters, Hughes holes up in a screening room in Hollywood for five months and endures a terrifying *interior* odyssey, and two short letters exchanged by Hughes and Peters during this time are enough to show us the once great man now completely fallen, the once great love now completely doomed.

American Airlines

One afternoon in September 1932, Howard Hughes got a close-cropped haircut at his hotel's barbershop, put on a department-store suit and, without a word to anyone, boarded a train going from Los Angeles to Fort Worth. The next day he stood in line at an American Airlines office to fill out an employment application, giving his name as Charles Howard. He was hired as a baggage handler and pilot trainee and did well, within three weeks getting a raise that doubled his salary.

One day Howard Hughes was in the chair and a man wearing a white suit walked in and asked for a haircut. Brookes told him it'd be ten or fifteen minutes so the man sat down for a shine. I jumped up and opened my kit—right away I smelled liquor on him. I rolled up his pants legs to keep them out of the polish and saw the tip of a pistol holster at his right ankle, but I didn't think anything about it. I'd seen them before.

I had finished one shoe and was starting the other when the man said, "You're Howard Hughes, aren't you?"

Hughes said he was.

"I auditioned for you when you were casting *Hell's Angels*," the man said. "An officer who said one line during the ballroom scene. 'It's less than I expected, but more than I hoped for.' When Jean Harlow walks by he says that about her dress. I had the part when Howard Hawks was directing, but when you took over I had to audition again and then suddenly"— the man snapped his fingers—"no more part."

"Sir, are you a guest here?" Brookes said.

"Don't I look good enough to be staying here?" the man said. "Room one thousand eighty-three. Call the desk."

"That's quite all right, sir," Brookes said.

"Damn," the man said.

"Hey," Hughes said. "He didn't mean anything."

"Why didn't you like my audition?" the man said.

"I remember you now," Hughes said.

"So what was it?"

"You were drunk," Hughes said.

"But I did my line okay."

"Yeah, but I didn't want a drunk on my soundstage."

"Watch out, boy," the man said and he leaned over in the chair and shoved me out of the way and unsnapped the holster and pulled the pistol out. It was a silver derringer. I hopped off the stand.

"What the hell?" Hughes said.

"Oh, God," Brookes said.

The man pointed the gun at me. "Lock the door and pull the shades." I did.

"Do you want money?" Hughes said and you could see his hands rustling underneath the apron. Then Brookes dropped his scissors and they clattered on the floor, everybody jumped, and the man jerked the pistol in the direction of the noise. Hughes ducked.

"Watch it," the man said.

Everybody stared at each other.

"What'd you want?" Hughes said.

The man sighted the pistol at Hughes and squinted one eye.

"If I did something to you I'm sorry," Hughes said. He kept scooting up in the chair, trying to move away somehow—he was practically standing up on the footrest. Brookes kept edging away from him with these little steps.

"Would you still like to be in *Hell's Angels*?" Hughes said.

"Very funny," the man said.

"We'll reshoot your scene and splice it in," Hughes said. "New prints can be made. We'll redo the credits."

"That would be just goddamn wonderful," the man said, "if you were telling the truth."

"I'm completely serious," Hughes said. His hands moved underneath the apron and he pulled out a business card. "Here. Call this number this afternoon. I'll set everything up. It'll be shot within the week."

"You're lying," the man said.

"If I say I'm going to do a thing, I do it," Hughes said.

"You said I had a job on *Hell's Angels*."

"No, Howard Hawks said you had a job."

The man finally lowered the pistol. He stepped off the shine stand and grabbed the card and looked at it.

"All right," he said. He switched the pistol to his left hand and held out his right one for Hughes to shake. Hughes didn't take it.

"I want a handshake," the man said.

"My word's my word," Hughes said.

"I said I want a handshake," the man said.

"If I'm lying a handshake isn't going to change anything," Hughes said.

"I'm not kidding," the man said. "Shake my hand."

"I can't," Hughes said.

"Why not?" the man said.

"I don't shake hands with anyone who's been drinking," Hughes said.

"What?" the man said.

"I'm sorry, but I just don't do that," Hughes said.

"That's crazy," the man said.

"Well, *crazy*'s a strong word," Hughes said. "I don't know if I'd call it that."

The man stared at Hughes like Hughes was some kind of

freak. I did too. I couldn't believe he wouldn't just go ahead and shake the guy's hand and get rid of him.

"You call that number this afternoon," Hughes said.

"I'm going to," the man said, "and if you're lying, I'll find you again. Count on that." He went to the door, then looked over his shoulder at Hughes and pointed the pistol at him. "Remember, I'll find you," he said. Then he stuck the pistol in his pants pocket, unlocked the door and left, half of one shoe still covered with polish.

"Christ, I'm calling security," Brookes said.

"No," Hughes said. "And I want you to do me a favor. Don't mention this to anyone."

"Mr. Hughes, I've got to notify—"

"Please don't," Hughes said, "and if anyone asks if I was here today I want you both to deny it."

"I don't understand," Brookes said.

"We've got to keep this quiet," Hughes said.

It took Hughes awhile to convince him, but finally Brookes agreed. Then he finished the haircut. He lathered up the back of Hughes's neck and used the razor. He toweled him off, then held up the mirror and moved it around the way barbers do so Hughes could approve. Hughes kept frowning as he looked at himself.

"Is everything satisfactory, Mr. Hughes?" Brookes asked.

"Cut it all off," Hughes said.

"Excuse me, sir?" Brookes said.

"Make me look like a plumber or welder or something. Like any man you might meet on the street."

"Are you sure, sir?" Brookes said.

"I'm sure," Hughes said.

I must find a woman who does not know me. After we are in love I will tell her who I am. If her attitude toward me stays the same then I will have found true love but if she starts asking for luxuries then I will have been deceived again.

Time is of the absolute essence. The actor today showed me that. He was a messenger telling me to change my path immediately. I had to look death in the face in an absolutely unexpected situation to be shocked enough to hear his message: Get away. Change your life. Time is of the essence.

People think I am the luckiest man on earth. But what if by some impossible freak of nature a wolf was born into a family of squirrels? How would that wolf feel when he tried to climb a tree or eat some acorns? Most would look at that wolf and think, what a lucky animal, he is so powerful among the squirrels. But what if this wolf wanted to sleep in a cave instead of a tree? Howl instead of squeak? What if he had to fight the constant maddening impulse to kill and eat the squirrels? That is the situation I find myself in. I am torn between being a pilot named Charles Howard for the rest of my life or possibly becoming Howard Hughes again at some point and developing Nevada after my own vision. Either way, this project I am embarking on will help me take one of these courses of action and will be a beginning on getting me out of my present circumstances.

Faces. That's what I want. I want to see them around the dinner table. One has come in second in the spelling bee. Another one pouts because she was teased while playing with the neighborhood children. Another one wants me to help him build a model airplane after dinner. Sometimes you stop and look around and ask yourself why am I making the most popular movies in America? Why am I building an aviation empire? Why am I dating and winning the world's most beautiful women? Why is Nevada important? Without faces it means nothing.

Joel Pym, reconstructed from Tom Lourdes's story notes
Hell's Angels wasn't out then, but they re-released it about a year later and I went to see it. Sure enough, there was the guy, saying the same line he'd said in the shop. You could tell the background in his shot was a little different than in the rest of the scene. But maybe you wouldn't have noticed if you didn't know what I did.

When the guy said his line he was grinning like he really had just seen Jean Harlow.

Alton Reece interview with Janice and Lisa Trundle at their home in Fort Worth, Texas

I arrive for the interview on a cloudy, overcast afternoon; the air is thick with the coming rain. I use the brass knocker, then wait outside the neat white clapboard house for what seems a long time; I'm almost ready to leave when Janice Trundle's daughter Lisa finally opens the door, and as she does rain begins falling in widely spaced splats.

Lisa Trundle is a tall, large-boned woman, probably forty-five, with long dirty-blond hair. She leads me down a hallway in which books are haphazardly stacked to waist height on both sides and into a living

room in which shelves of books cover the walls—the house looks like
an untidy used-book store. Janice Trundle, dressed in a quilted dark
blue housecoat, her white hair noticeably thinning, sits in a wheelchair,
reading. When I enter she looks up at me and her glasses are so thick
her eyes look huge, startling. She doesn't say hello when her daughter
introduces me, but just stares at me, expressionless. The air in the close
dim room is warm and musty. Clear plastic is draped over much of the
furniture. I sit on the love seat, the plastic crinkling loudly, and Lisa
sits down next to me. I smile at Janice Trundle, but she just continues
to stare at me blankly with her huge-looking eyes.

AR: Mrs. Trundle, thanks for seeing me.

JT: *(She closes the book in her lap, and I see that it is Marcus*
Aurelius's Meditations. *She nods at her daughter.)* She liked
your book about Melville. She's the one who wanted to
meet you.

LT: Actually I did. I thought your book was the most interesting
thing I'd read in a long time.

AR: Thank you.

JT: I didn't care for it. It was too scattered for my taste.

LT: *(Rolling her eyes.)* Yes, Mother prefers Galsworthy-type
romanticism. English countrysides with flowers growing in
the characters' ears, their underwear—wherever they have
enough moisture to flourish.

JT: I think Galsworthy's horrid. You know that.

AR: *(I clear my throat.)* Mrs. Trundle, on the telephone Lisa told
me that in order to do this interview, you insisted it be used
in its entirety or not at all. Did anyone call you about our
interview?

LT: Yes, yes, this man named Tom Lourdes called her. I begged her not to listen to him.

AR: All right. I just wondered.

JT: *(A faint smile on her lips.)* Even if Lourdes hadn't called, I'd have made sure we had that agreement. I read the article about you in *People,* and I don't—

LT: Dammit, Mother, stop. Just don't go there.

AR: *(I put my notepad down on the coffee table.)* You know, I can see this probably isn't going to work out. We should just stop before we waste any—

LT: *(Touching my arm.)* No, please, stay. I don't think . . . say, are you okay?

AR: I'm fine.

LT: You're sure?

(I nod.)

LT: You know, I don't know why people are such vultures when it comes to knowing about the private lives of talented people like yourself. And the IRS, everybody knows what they're like—they punish success, and I'm sure that's why they're after you.

(I nod again.)

LT: You know, I can tell you anything you want to know. You won't have to deal with *her* at all. *(She gives her mother a dirty look.)* God knows I heard this enough growing up. She'd tell me the story of the great Charles Howard at bedtime like it was a fairy tale. She'd even bring him up to my father. She always let him know he never made her as happy as the great Charles Howard did. She broke his heart. Put him in an early grave.

JT: *(She clears her throat, and then in a phlegmy voice.)* The price of a fifth of whiskey going up to three dollars is what killed him.

LT: Mother, if you're not going to be helpful, just be quiet, okay? You've already shared enough of your negativity for one day. *(She smiles at me.)* Now, let's see, where to start? She was working as a cigarette girl on a train. She was twenty-two—

JT: Twenty.

LT: Twenty, then. She always said Hughes was about the handsomest man she'd ever seen, but she didn't recognize him because she didn't read movie magazines. He was dressed in a brown suit that was too big for him and was writing in a leather-bound journal. She stood there with that tray she carried and asked him if he wanted anything, and when he looked up at her, he looked angry that she was bothering him.

JT: *(Impatiently.)* No, he didn't. He looked shy.

LT: *(She sighs.)* So, she asked him if he wanted anything and he said no. Then she asked him what he was writing. He just said his ideas and didn't elaborate, but as they kept talking he told her he was going to Fort Worth to try to get a job with American Airlines. Then he asked for a Hershey bar. When he reached up to pay, the price tag for his suit was hanging off his sleeve. Mother used the scissors she kept in the tray for trimming cigars and cut it off for him.

AR: Did he pursue her after they got to Fort Worth?

LT: Oh, he didn't wait that long. Apparently she saw him a few minutes later in another car, walking down the aisle toward her. He asked her for another Hershey bar, then asked her if she'd like to eat supper with him on her break. She had to say no because they weren't allowed to fraternize with passengers, but she told him they could have a meal together in Fort Worth.

AR: So did they get together that evening?

JT: *(Smiling faintly.)* Of course not. Women weren't such rutting whores *then*.

LT: *(She rolls her eyes, then touches my arm and leans toward me.)* Listen, she has always just *insisted* he never touched her, except to kiss her good night. *(She makes the* OK *sign.)* Right. And according to her, *every* time he came to see her he had some piece of junk for a gift.

JT: It wasn't junk.

LT: A puppet of the Mad Hatter? *(She raises her eyebrows.)* If that's not junk, what is? Purple pebbles he found in a streambed? A block of wood he'd carved to look like a locomotive? All junk.

AR: Do you still have any of those things?

LT: No, she got drunk one night when I was a child and burned them all. All she's got left is the engagement ring he gave her. It's in a lockbox down at the bank. It's really in amazingly poor taste. *(She wrinkles her nose as if smelling something rotten.)* A ten-carat diamond for a center stone, with twenty-one smaller diamonds and twenty-one rubies clustered around it. I had it appraised three years ago and the man priced it between two hundred and fifty and three hundred thousand, but it still looks like it came out of a gumball machine.

AR: I'd like to see it, if it's possible.

JT: *(Sharply.)* No.

LT: *(With a droll smile.)* My name's on the signature card, Mother.

AR: Didn't that ring seem like a red flag that Hughes might not be who he said he was?

LT: Oh, he had a lie to explain the ring, but I'm getting ahead of myself. The time leading up to when he gave her the ring, apparently he just about lived in this house. She always said Hughes became fast friends with her parents. Maybe that's true, but I always suspected she just said that to hurt my father, because he didn't get along with her family—they thought he was beneath her. He was a ticket clerk at the railway station. He'd been asking her out for a long time and getting nowhere, but after Hughes dumped her she ran to him.

JT: *(Livid.)* My parents thought the *world* of Charles, don't you ever doubt that! He and Father were always out back working on father's old cars. *(Her face is red.)* He'd . . . he'd help my mother make the ice cream every night, too. Those were just *wonderful* times.

AR: So how did the engagement take place?

LT: He asked her to marry him the day after Thanksgiving, while they were taking a walk here in the neighborhood. When he asked her there wasn't any big romantic moment, he just handed her the ring and then started talking about its history right away, covering his tracks. He said his father had been a card shark and had won the ring from a timber baron in a poker game up in Vancouver.

JT: That's not how it happened.

LT: Then what'd he do, Mother? Ride in on a white horse and climb your hair to the top of the tower?

JT: *(She eyes her daughter with a cool, detached, superior expression.)* I'll tell you what happened. We were walking, and it was chilly. I had forgotten to put on a sweater, so Charles took off his pilot's jacket and gave it to me—he was still wearing his uniform because he had just come in from a flight. After I put on the jacket he told me to check its side pocket. I reached in and pulled out a ring box. I opened it, and he said, "You can wear that if you want to."

AR: So how'd the engagement get broken off?

LT: He just dumped her.

JT: That's another lie, but it's what she tells herself to make herself feel better, since no one's ever asked her. What Charles said was that his time with me had been the happiest days of his life and he didn't want to break up, but he was doing it for my own good because life as Howard Hughes wasn't normal and he didn't want to put me through that. He was crying like a baby.

LT: Yes, he called her on the telephone from Cleveland. It was a very touching scene.

AR: Okay. *(Short pause.)* Well, I don't have any more questions.

LT: Would you like to see the room Hughes slept in when he stayed over here? It's my room now.

AR: Sure, okay.

JT: No. Absolutely not.

LT: Just be quiet, Mother.

144

I have asked Janice to marry me but I still cannot make myself tell her who I am. I gave her the ring for the express purpose of using its appearance as an opening to reveal to her that I am Howard Hughes, but then I just could not do it. The longer this deception continues the greater her sense of betrayal will be when I do tell her. It is probably already too late. I will probably lose her now no matter what I do.

I like being Charles Howard. If there was just some way to really become him. It could be done, I think. It would entail selling absolutely everything, the tool company, the real estate, all of it. There would be some publicity but I don't think I would have to appear in the public eye at any time to accomplish this so Janice would never find out. But would this truly work? Someone like me giving away all I have would be like Alexander the Great conquering the world and then giving it back. It would be unheard of. Historic. Such a thing has never been done on the scale it would be if I did it. Has one of the richest people in the world ever given away all he had and then lived a normal life? For the life of me I cannot think of one so I guess it has never happened because if it had his name would be on everyone's lips in an instant like Lincoln's.

I have to decide whether I am going to take one of the most historic steps in human history.

O. C. Mennick, pilot with American Airlines, 1931–1953,
reconstructed from Tom Lourdes's story notes
We made eight, ten flights a week together for four months and during that time I had no idea he was actually Howard Hughes.

The day the truth finally came out, we were on a flight between Fort Worth and Cleveland. I was ribbing him about getting married and asked him if they had set a date. He said no.

"You will soon," I said. "A girl wants to get that settled so she can plan things."

He shrugged.

"Don't tell me she hasn't mentioned it," I said.

"She has," he said, "but just in a very general way. We've got a lot of things that need working out first. It's going to be a while."

"Don't count on it, buddy," I said. "It's like a fever with them once they decide to do it."

Then he changed the subject completely. He asked me if I'd ever been to Nevada. I told him I hadn't.

"Well, big things are getting ready to happen there," he said.

"Is some kind of development going on?" I asked.

"Not right now," he said, "but I've been thinking about Nevada a lot and I want to talk to you about it. I think two fellows like you and me could go out there and accomplish some things." Then he talked about starting an airline and basing it in Nevada. He wanted me to go in with him. At first it would be local, but he saw the business eventually growing into an international enterprise.

"Do you know how much it costs to start an airline?" I said. "And what about customers? Where would you take them in Nevada? From one patch of cactus to another?"

That's when he told me his scheme of building golf courses as tourist attractions. Before he finished I was laughing.

"Let's say all this would work out," I said. "How're you going to pay for it all?"

"Investors," he said.

"Who would invest in such a scheme?" I asked.

"For your information, I've already got a fellow who's interested," he said. "A very wealthy person."

"Who?" I said.

"I can't say," he said. "He wants to remain anonymous right now."

I said, "Have you talked to Janice about all this?"

"No," he said.

"Well, maybe you better," I said.

"I'm certain she'll support me in whatever I do," he said.

I didn't say anything else. I let it drop because I could tell he was getting steamed.

In Cleveland, we got the passengers and their baggage unloaded and got the plane squared away and then went into the American office to do our paperwork. Some regional managers were visiting that day and that was slowing things down, and a couple of other crews were in line ahead of us, and as we stood there Charles picked up a movie magazine one of the secretaries had on her desk and thumbed through it. Suddenly he said, "I'll be damned."

"What is it?" I said.

"Ginger Rogers is free again," he said.

That seemed an odd thing to say, but I didn't ask him about it. Finally we reached the counter and both of us handed across our paperwork to the fellow there, and he went back to a filing cabinet to get some forms he had to complete. The visiting managers were standing in a group near the back of the room, talking and laughing. Charles tapped me on the arm and pointed to one of them and said, "That's Roger Eckheart, the guy who runs the northeast. He's an idiot."

"How do you know him?" I asked.

"He was at the New York premiere of *Hell's Angels*," he said.

"*You* were at *that?*" I said.

"I was between flying jobs and worked security at it," he said. "You seen the movie?"

"Yeah," I said.

"What'd you think?" he asked.

"It was all right," I said, "but I know a pilot in Indiana who had a pilot friend who worked on it, and he said that Hughes fellow didn't hesitate to ask pilots to take crazy risks. He said Hughes treated pilots like so much meat."

"I heard he took the same risks himself," he said. "He had a bad crash doing a stunt. Almost killed him."

"Well then, he got some of his own medicine," I said. "Three pilots died making that movie."

"Why're you so down on Howard Hughes?" he said.

"Because he's a spoiled rich boy," I said. "He's got more money than sense. Didn't that movie cost two or three million dollars?"

"Four," he said.

"That's what I mean," I said. "He was spending Daddy's money, so he didn't care. You wait and see. He'll go bankrupt. Then he'll know what it's like to be out here making a living."

His expression turned blank. I asked if something was wrong. He shook his head, then wanted to know what I'd think if a fellow like Hughes were to give away all his money.

"That's a good one," I said.

"Just say he did," he said. "What would you think?"

"I'd think he was a fool," I said.

He nodded. Then the fellow came back with our forms and we signed off. I started away from the counter but Charles didn't move. He took off his uniform hat and said loudly, "Hey, Eckheart."

Everyone in the group of managers stopped talking and looked at him. A short well-dressed man said, "Yes, what is it?"

"I'm going to put your shitty airline out of business," Charles said.

All talking in the room stopped and everyone looked at Charles. Eckheart took a couple of steps toward the counter, his eyes narrowed. "Hughes?" he said.

"Yeah," he said.

"What in God's name?" Eckheart asked.

Charles didn't say anything. He just turned and walked out.

I found him in a hangar, sitting on a workbench and staring at the floor. I felt awful about the things I'd said. I said, "Hey there. Charles," and his head jerked up. "Call me Howard," he said.

"Right, okay," I said.

"So *Hell's Angels* . . . so I'm a butcher, am I? That's the general consensus among pilots?"

"I don't know," I said.

"I'm going to break every damn aviation record there is,"

he said. "Let's see what you say then. And I'm going to build an airline that makes American look like the third-rate outfit it is."

Even though he was sharp with me, I told him I had enjoyed flying with him and that I thought he was an excellent pilot. When he had calmed down a little I asked him why he was so angry at Eckheart.

"At the premiere party in New York I found him kissing Jean Harlow in the cloakroom," he said.

That was the last time I saw him. He didn't make the return flight with me to Fort Worth that afternoon and the next day in Cleveland they took publicity photos of him handling baggage and sitting in a cockpit looking out the side window. The whole thing became a newspaper story for a day or two.

Hughes diary entry, December 21, 1933

If things were different it would have been wonderful with Janice but things are not different and you cannot cry about what is not and never will be. I have learned you cannot fulfill a great purpose like the building of Nevada and make ice cream on the front porch every night too.

Why isn't Ginger returning my calls?

Alton Reece interview with Lisa Trundle at the airport Ramada Inn in Dallas, Texas

Lisa Trundle arrives at my motel room wearing a gauzy white summer dress and a wide-brimmed floppy straw hat that has a colorful scarf as a hatband. She smells faintly of patchouli. We sit at the card table and she begins by saying she'd like our conversation to be used in the book, and used word for word, too—she doesn't want her mother to get better treatment than she does. I acquiesce because that's about all I can do, but inwardly I roil at what these self-serving demands for complete transcriptions are doing to my book. I pour two glasses of wine.

AR: *(Forcing a smile.)* So, did you bring the ring?

LT: *(She sips her wine.)* It's in my bag.

AR: My lawyer faxed me a copy of the release he drew up. *(I point to it on the table.)* We can get it notarized down at the concierge desk.

LT: What's your hurry?

AR: No hurry.

LT: *(Smiling, flirty.)* You know, if I let you take this ring, I want something in return. *(She makes a production of looking around the room; her eyes finally fix on Hughes's fedora, lying on the bed.)* I want you to put this hat on. I love neat old hats like this. Where'd you get this? *(She leans forward in her chair and picks up the hat, examines it a moment, then reaches across the table and puts it on my head. She sits back and sizes me up.)* You look cute. *(Then she reaches in her bag, pulls out a postcard-size manila envelope that has a bulge in the center, opens it and pours the ring out into her hand. She holds it out and I reach for it, but she pulls it back.)*

AR: Well?

LT: *(Coyly.)* Not yet.

AR: *(I lean forward in the chair and sit with my elbows on my knees, staring at the coach-and-horse pattern that decorates the bedspread, hundreds of little brown coaches and horses in perfect rows. I take off the hat and toss it on the bed.)* Look, this isn't your problem, but this book . . . I can't stick just anything in it, okay? We need to get this business of ours done.

LT: *(Again coyly.)* So does your wife ever travel with you?

(I don't answer. I stare blankly across the room.)

LT: Well?

AR: You read the article in *People,* didn't you?

LT: *(Holding up the ring in front of her face, toying with it, watching the light glint off it.)* You know, I think what you're doing, following in Hughes's footsteps, going where he went, meeting the people who knew him, I think it makes perfect sense. Faulkner lived his whole life in Yoknapatawpha, so to speak. *(She stops looking at the ring and looks at me. She smiles.)* Proust, he actually stayed in bed, didn't he?

(I nod.)

LT: *(She reaches for the recorder.)* Where's the button?

AR: Here.

The Box

On May 16, 1943, Howard Hughes awoke at four in the morning, Ava Gardner still asleep beside him, and drove from their hotel in Reno to Lake Mead. His modification of the Sikorsky amphibian airplane for military use was one of the few wartime projects he'd had approved, and he was testing the plane that morning for government inspectors. Hughes had made 4,588 landings in the Sikorsky on Lake Mead during six months of testing; however, on this day, he didn't know his ground crew had forgotten to load tail ballast, the weight of which would keep the nose of the plane from tipping over into the water on touchdown. Hughes had four passengers, two inspectors and two of his own mechanics. At his best, Hughes probably could've controlled the plane even without the ballast, but that day he wasn't at his best, and one man drowned in the crash and another died from the injuries he received. Hughes himself refused medical treatment. Instead, his clothes soaked in his and his passengers' blood, he insisted he be taken to a local department store to buy new ones, then insisted on flying to California that very minute so he could inform his mechanic's wife in person that her husband was dead. Witnesses in the airplane, piloted by Hughes, said he kept whispering over and over, "My fault."

As soon as the Sikorsky was recovered and restored, Hughes took off in it on a rambling eighteen-month trip. For seven months he traveled in a triangle among Las Vegas, Palm Springs, and Reno, and then he went to Louisiana, Florida, and finally New York City, and everywhere he went he took with him a six-foot-long box that was shaped like an old six-sided wood coffin. This box was constructed of the thick cardboard used for concrete forms and was always covered in brown wrapping paper tied with string. Those who traveled with Hughes said it weighed at least 150 pounds, though they didn't know what was in it, and Hughes adamantly refused to tell them.

Hughes memo dated July 7, 1944, and titled "Care And Handling Of The Box"

1. The box is never to be opened.
2. Keep in our emergency kit at all times a roll of Number

7 brown butcher paper, plenty of Number 12 string, and a canister of glue.

3. If a small tear develops in the paper you are to cut a patch that adequately covers the tear and secure it with glue. Under no circumstances unwrap the box. If the box is soaked in a rain shower, inform me immediately. If I am not available, leave the box alone until I return.

4. If a porter or taxi driver asks what is in the box reply that that information is confidential and classified, a part of the war effort.

5. Defend the box with your life.

6. When situating the box on the bed in its room, remove the pillows from the bed, then position the box in the exact equicenter of the bed using a T square.

7. Next, take the telephone off the hook. Draw the curtains together and tape them where they meet so that no light, not even the tiniest shaft, falls into the room and possibly on the box from that aperture. Tape the bottom and the left and right borders of the curtains to the window trim. This should leave light coming into the room only at the top. At this point in the procedure, the room has grown very dark. Switch on the lamp farthest from the box so that the least light possible falls on it. Using finish nails, tack up the large blackout curtain over the whole window to create a double barrier to light. Turn off the lamp. If you see absolutely any light, the smallest amount you can imagine, use tape to patch the leak. When the room is in total darkness when the lamp is off as if you are a blind man, the job is done.

8. Leave the room and lock it. Yank the knob three times to make sure the door is locked.

9. Check the box on this schedule: 6 a.m., 12 Noon, 6 p.m., Midnight. Make any needed repairs to the curtains.

10. The room where the box is kept is not to have maid service. First, when checking in, inform the front desk that room number —, wherever we are keeping the box, is not to have maid service. Second, hang the Do Not Disturb sign on the doorknob of the room. Third, discover the usual working patterns of the maids, and when they approach the room, you are to be standing there, smiling, saying, "Thanks, but we don't need maid service. My wife can take care of it." Accept towels and linens if she offers them, but if she acts as if she is going to enter the room despite your wishes, manhandle her away from the door.

11. I will conduct periodic surprise inspections of the room to make sure my instructions are being carried out in a professional manner.

Alton Reece interview with Johnny Russelli, mechanic at Hughes Aircraft, 1939–1956, at the Days Inn on the outskirts of Palm Springs, California

Johnny Russelli lives in a retirement community in Palm Desert, a short drive from Palm Springs, and although I offer to come to his home to interview him, he says he needs to come into Palm Springs anyway to take care of some business, so we can just meet at my motel. On the morning we've agreed to, he knocks on my room door at exactly 11 A.M.

155

I answer and we shake hands. He's a tall, burly man who, despite his age, still gives an impression of strength. He wears neatly pressed khaki pants, a blue button-up shirt, and works an unlit, sweet-smelling cigar in the corner of his mouth. He enters the room, then stops and stares at the box on the bed.

JR: This isn't the one Boss had, is it?

(I nod.)

JR: Yeah? So what's going on?

AR: Nothing.

JR: *(He approaches the box and lays a hand on it.)* Has it still got the same stuff in it?

(A short silence.)

AR: I was under the impression Hughes was the only one who knew what was in it.

JR: Yeah, that was true for a long time, but one day I was moving this thing by myself and it broke open because the cardboard had gotten wet. It was full of douche bags. Dozens of them, all shapes, colors, and sizes, and comic books, too, a couple hundred of them, mostly *Red Ryder's*. *(He grins and shakes his head.)* I managed to get everything back together before Boss found out.

AR: Well, okay. Let's sit down. *(We both sit at the card table.)* First thing, Mr. Russelli, I want to thank you for taking the time to talk to me. Now, I know you worked closely with Hughes a number of times, and the first one I wanted to ask you about was a day you and Myron Tompkins did some work on a Mercedes as a practical joke. Do you remember that?

JR: *(Staring at the box.)* Yeah.

AR: Anything to say about that?

JR: *(He shrugs.)* Not really.

AR: *(Short pause.)* Okay. Well then, I know you and Tompkins accompanied him for much of the trip where he carried the box. What was that like?

JR: *(Still staring at the box, distracted.)* Different.

AR: Can you elaborate?

JR: *(He doesn't answer. Instead, he leans forward in his chair, reaches over and taps the box.)* This couldn't be the same box. It looks too new. The one we had was real beat up, even back then. *(He sits back in his chair and looks at me.)* Mr. Reece, I hate to be the one to tell you, but someone's misled you. We handled that box too much for it to have lasted this long. Every day at three in the afternoon, we had to have a taxi loaded with all the luggage, including the box. If Boss decided to leave, we checked out and drove to the plane. If he decided to stay, we unloaded, unpacked, and then set up the box again according to these instructions we had, which from the way you got this room rigged, I can see you know about.

AR: Didn't Hughes make Tompkins get false teeth during this trip?

JR: Uh, yeah, he did.

AR: Did Hughes say why he wanted him to get them?

JR: Not that I can remember.

AR: All right. Do you remember a time when you went to Las Vegas with Hughes and left Tompkins in Reno with the box?

JR: *(He nods.)* He wanted me to go with him to meet some people on business.

AR: Was Tompkins upset about being left behind?

JR: *(An amused smile.)* No, he didn't mind staying. He had a different maid he was seeing at all the hotels where we stayed.

AR: What happened at the meeting?

JR: Well, Bugsy Siegel was there, and the governor of the state, too. Boss was talking about building golf courses and aircraft plants and Siegel was laying out plans for casinos. Siegel said the state didn't have enough room for both their plans. He was threatening Boss in a very polite way, and Boss just stood up and walked out.

AR: How did Hughes react to this disappointment?

JR: He acted pretty beat.

AR: Didn't you and Tompkins abandon him not long after this?

JR: *(His brow furrowed.)* It was Christmas, for chrissakes, and he wouldn't give us time off. My wife was raising hell and so was Tompkins's. We hadn't been home for five months. So sure, we left, and sure, I felt bad about it. Christmas Eve was Boss's birthday. But I left a note under his door, telling him we'd be back the day after Christmas.

AR: I'm sorry, I really meant no offense, Mr. Russelli, it's just that I've grown very interested lately in that part of the human psyche that makes us abandon, almost by instinct, those who're suffering great misfortune. Ever notice how as soon as things start going wrong for you, people start avoiding you, yet, at the same time, they're almost sexually excited by your suffering? That's the blood lust in us, and when you get right down to it, most human behavior can be explained by blood lust. The psychologists, the sociologists, the philosophers, the theologians, they've all got their little theories, but down deep, we all know there's only one thing that's true: this life is a straight cash business. What do people really care about, no matter what they say? Do churchgoers sell their SUVs and drive Escorts so they can feed starving people? Do liberals who profess to be so worried about the good of humankind give up their cell phones and ski trips? See? You can sing all the hymns you want, but blood lust isn't ever going away. We just refine it. We kill with words now instead of swords. We make phone calls and ruin careers. We get divorce lawyers. We've got a legally sanctioned band of thugs called the IRS who seize assets without a trial. We convict innocent men in the court of *Hard Copy* and *People* magazine and the mincing, gutless, self-righteous prosecutors of this kind of bloodless assassination all cover themselves by saying, "We just want the truth," when everyone knows that's a lie, they really just want the same things everyone else wants—money, fame, sex, Mommy and Daddy's approval, or, no, most likely, they're just trying to cover up their own sins by raving about someone else's. Do you see what I'm saying, Mr. Russelli? We no longer have the courage to strike our enemies with the strength of our arms. We use our tongues, like women. Don't you agree?

(Johnny Russelli then stands up and mentions the other appointment he has to keep, so I thank him for his time and see him out.)

Hughes diary entry, December 25, 1944
Sometimes you would rather stick needles in your eyes than live

one more day with the mindless bastards you have to put up with. I can't believe the arrogant mediocrities who govern this state are acquiescing to these gangsters and giving their blessing to a scheme that will turn this place into a national joke of vice and corruption and the un-American principle you don't have to work for what you get. Mark my words. This is the beginning of the end for this country.

Gambling, in and of itself, doesn't seem so bad—on the surface. Most people will not think past this surface because most people don't think twice about anything because they are too busy with what they're putting in their mouths or what's going on between their legs. Because of this gambling will take hold and in fifty years it will be as much a part of the national landscape and as widely accepted as baseball. Then we will be in a hell of a shape.

This Bugsy Siegel, you know he's around because you start smelling the hair oil two minutes before he comes into view. I cannot believe after all these years of planning and hoping to turn Nevada into a thriving place with an aviation industry producing good jobs, a state that would be home to a great city, a port to the heavens, it is instead going to be a Sodom and Gomorrah full of germ-ridden whores and games of chance. I just never thought something like this could happen. It seems so out of the realm of possibility, the stupidity on such a grand scale, I never considered it a contingency I needed to prepare for.

All my work the last several months has been a cruel joke played by fate. Well, fine, but the real estate I have bought in Nevada will never be sold in my lifetime. The only way I would sell was if Siegel bent over and kissed my ass at Carnegie

Hall on a Saturday night. . . . [At this point in the diary entry, Hughes devotes roughly three-quarters of a page to a freehand technical drawing. I suspected it might have something to do with airplanes, so I had an aviation engineer examine it and he said it was a rough outline of a type of hydraulic steering system for large airplanes that wasn't invented until the 1960s, twenty years after Hughes apparently envisioned it. The text that follows is the rest of the entry for December 25, 1944, which begins again directly below the drawing—ed.]

I offered to bring their goddamn families to Las Vegas for Christmas. I planned a large party with a wonderfully decorated tree and toys for their children but Russelli said his wife insisted on having Christmas at home. So I get back to my room and see a note on the floor and at first think it is part of some birthday surprise they have planned but then open it and find out different so I call the desk and rent a car and it was an hour before the goddamn thing arrived and when it did it was a station wagon. I called the desk and complained but they said it was Christmas and it was hard to get the right car.

I drove through the desert in a silence so complete I might as well have been dead. Outside Beverly Hills I ran out of gas. I started walking. I walked until I reached Cary's [Cary Grant's—ed.] bungalow at dawn. I had hoped he'd say happy birthday Howard when he saw me but he just opened the door and stumbled back to bed. I got a glass of water and stood there drinking it and looking at his tree. It was tall and very full and green and covered with gold and silver statuettes of elves and reindeer and religious figures and stained glass hangings and balls made of frosted glass. Plenty of gifts.

I lifted off a stained glass hanging of Mary holding the infant Jesus and put it in my pocket. I have never understood this Jesus business but Christmas is Christmas so I opened one of the smaller presents addressed to Cary: a silver pocket comb in a leather case. I went to the bathroom and washed my face and used the comb, then put it back in its case and put it in my pocket.

I left the bungalow and walked for a long time. The stained glass ornament was too big for my pocket and jabbed my thigh. I tried to situate it better but could not so I carried it in my hand until I came to a church. It was very early, maybe eight or nine, and everything was dead because of Christmas but already music and shouting were coming from inside the church. I put the ornament on the top step where someone interested in Jesus could find it. I was several steps down the sidewalk when someone shouted Hey, is this yours? Did you drop this? No I said. He held up the ornament and looked at it. He was smoking a cigarette. Sure is pretty he said. Well it's yours now I said. Why don't you come in and join us? he said. We are going to have breakfast after the service. Eggs, coffee, hash browns, hotcakes, the whole works. We even got bacon off the black market. You hungry?

Inside children were running everywhere like frightened ants. Two guitar players played while the minister shouted and wept. People shouted, waved their arms, and hugged. I sat down at the end of a pew. The man sat down with me. What's your name? he asked. Howard Hughes I said and then he asked where I lived. I told him I had just come from Nevada. Home for Christmas? he asked. No I said. What do you do in Nevada? he asked. I told him I had hoped to start an airline and other aviation projects but that it was not working out. He looked at me funny. He said friend have you met Jesus? I said no. He said Jesus can release any demon that might be bothering you. Well I said. He put his hand on my shoulder, closed his eyes and started praying out loud. After a short time other men noticed and started walking toward me. The man stopped praying and told me to close my eyes. I did. I felt another hand on my shoulder. Soon hands were on my head, back, neck. They all prayed out loud. I opened my eyes. The men all had their eyes closed. They were smiling. I counted nine of them. I started getting uncomfortable. I shrugged my shoulders and twisted and ducked my head but each hand just pressed harder and I heard an urgency come into their voices. I tried to stand up but the hands pushed me down. The man opened his eyes. Do not fight he said. His expression was sincere. Thanks I said but it would be better for you fellows to get on with your service so we can get finished and eat. This is the service he said. I tried to stand up again and this time all the hands pushed me back so that I was laying on the pew. Relax the man said. Nothing good will happen if you fight.

I decided to lay there a minute because I was exhausted by the long drive and all the walking so I closed my eyes and I must have fallen asleep because the next thing I knew they were all gone and I was lying there by myself. I sat up. I heard voices from below. The room was gray, just some light coming through the windows. At the front of the church was a painting of Jesus with a huge bloody red heart encircled by thorns. I kept staring at that. Soon the man appeared in the doorway behind the podium. Hello I said. I fell asleep. Yes he said. We tried to wake you but could not. We have saved you two plates of food downstairs he said. Come down and eat. Thanks I said but I probably should be going. No, come and eat he said, and you are welcome to come home with me and spend the day with my family. We are going to have another big meal this evening. I know how it is to be on the road he said. I hitched out here from Oklahoma years ago. What do you do? I asked him. Dig graves he said. That is necessary work I said. Yes he said. Say, tell me something I said. How do you believe in all this business? Jesus and all this? I do not know exactly he said. I did not used to. I saw my father kill himself with a shotgun when we lost our farm. I was walking to the barn and I saw him in the passthrough put it to his mouth and pull the trigger. My brother and sister both died of the typhoid not long after. Then my mother lost her head. That is when I started west. I would curse God every morning when I woke up. If I saw a Bible I would spit on it. I hope the Lord forgives all that. So how did things change for you? I said. I am interested. I would like to know. They just did he said. One day I was going to get a bottle and walked in here instead. I got prayed over. Something happened. I cannot explain it. Look, why don't you come down and eat with us?

No, I am going. But before I do, do you know who I am? Do you know who Howard Hughes the aviator is? I am him. Yes I know he said. I did not recognize you at first, but I put it together soon enough.

Did you tell the rest? I asked. No he said. What would be the point?

I was pretty damn hungry so I did go down and eat the food

164

they saved. It was very good country-type food. They were opening presents and playing games.

What a terrible Christmas.

Ashley Roth, field agent for the FBI, 1942–1949, reconstructed from Tom Lourdes's story notes

Most defense manufacturers of a certain size were watched, standard procedure during the war. Hughes wasn't heavily into the war effort, but Hoover didn't like him and he wanted him watched anyway. It was my job to do that in Reno.

Hughes had this large, coffin-shaped box that he took with him everywhere—other agents in other cities reported it, too. Weeks passed and none of our agents got a chance to examine it. Some believed the box might contain uranium, that Hughes was getting involved in the atomic area, and one agent thought he might have murdered one of his girlfriends and the box held her corpse, and that idea was taken seriously, too. Hughes was known to be a jealous man.

Hughes traveled with two mechanics and without fail they all traveled together. Then one day Hughes left Reno in his airplane, but he took with him only one of the mechanics and he didn't take the box with him. I reported this, and received word back I should try to examine the box, since it would be easier to do with just one of Hughes's party there. So that afternoon I waited until I saw the mechanic who'd been left behind, the little one, leave his room and go down the street. I went first to Hughes's room, but the box wasn't there. Everything was normal enough, except there were at least a hundred bars of soap in the bathroom. He had a lot of books, mostly technical manuals about airplanes, soil management, and the design of golf courses. I also found notebooks filled with typical diary stuff and a lot of sketches of airplanes and some drawings of golf holes with degree-of-slope numbers penciled in.

I checked the mechanics' room next—the box wasn't there, and then I went to the third room. I used the skeleton key and opened the door and in the light that fell into the room I saw the box I was looking for, but on the bed beside it a heavy naked woman was lying back and at her feet was the little mechanic, wearing a shirt but no pants, right in the middle of climbing up on her. His head jerked around and he looked at me, his eyes huge and terrified in the dark like a possum's. The woman started screaming in Spanish and then the mechanic reached into his shirt pocket and threw something at me and right before it hit me in the forehead I saw teeth. Before I could react he was on me. He kicked me in the groin, yanked me into the room and slammed the door. Then it was completely dark. I couldn't see anything. I was in a good bit of pain, too, from where he'd kicked me. The woman was still screaming. He yelled, "Silencio!" in this countrified voice and she stopped. Then there was only the sound of his heavy breathing and the woman sniffling.

"I knew I shouldn'ta let her talk me into this," he said. "Now I'm gonna get my ass shot off in Jay-pan."

I could tell he was standing right over me.

"She did. She talked me into it," he said. "She can talk enough English to do that. She said the maids was goin' on about why they couldn't come in this room. She thought it'd be excitin' to

166

come in here and have our fun." He moaned. "Oh God, please don't tell him."

I reached underneath my jacket and took my revolver out. I undid the safety, which made a loud click.

"Did you hear that?" I said. "Do you know what it is?"

"Yessir."

"Turn on the lamp."

"Can I put on my trousers first?"

"Yes." I sat up with my back against the door. The light came on. The woman had pulled the bedspread up over herself, and he was standing next to the lamp. He looked to be near tears.

"Please don't tell him," he said. "Mr. Hughes could end my draft deferment . . . he . . . he could have me a ball-turret gunner in three days if that's what he wanted—my size, that's what they're gonna make me and those sons-of-bitches don't live as long as flies."

"What's in that box?" I asked him.

"I'd as lief tell you as not, but I don't know."

I raised my revolver to let him know I meant business. "Tell me."

"I don't know. I swear it."

I stood up. I had to crouch a little from where he had kicked me. I decided to use his belief I worked for Hughes to my advantage. "All right, I won't tell him I found you in here with this woman," I said, "if you open that box and let me look in it."

He looked at me a long moment. Then the next thing I knew the light was off and something hit me with great force. My revolver flew out of my hand and then he hit me again and

167

knocked me into a wall. I couldn't see him but I could hear him bouncing around the room and crashing into things. The woman started screaming again. I got on my hands and knees and groped for my revolver. He hit me several times. Finally I groped until I found the doorknob and got out of there.

In my report I said I'd never gotten an opportunity to examine the box. A week later I staged a burglary of my apartment and called the police to cover the loss of my revolver.

Until Hughes came back, the little mechanic didn't leave that room. He was in there for three days. There was no food delivered, nothing. The door never opened.

Alton Reece interview with Ashley Roth at his duplex in the Hill Valley retirement community in Reno, Nevada

I'm an hour and twenty-five minutes late for my meeting with Ashley Roth; that morning as I load the box into the cargo area of my station wagon I rip a foot-long gash in its wrapping paper and it takes twenty minutes to repair; then, as I'm pulling out of the motel parking lot, my muffler comes loose and starts dragging the ground. I drive down a four-lane for a half mile, throwing sparks, until I see a strip mall with a hardware store. I have to wait fifteen minutes for the store to open so I can buy wire, and then I spend another half hour under the car bracing up the loose muffler.

When I finally arrive at Ashley Roth's residence, he is apparently watching out a window because before I am halfway up his sidewalk he comes outside and stands on his front stoop, holding a baseball bat diagonally across his chest with two hands the way a soldier holds a rifle. Where am I going with that box? he asks. I lower the hand truck and apologize for being late, explain what happened, and then I assure him everything is fine, there's nothing dangerous about the box. Put it back in your wagon he says. You're not bringing it inside.

I reload the box into the wagon, then follow Mr. Roth into his duplex, which is bright and airy, with tall ceilings and lots of windows. He sits on the couch and leans the baseball bat against the armrest. He nods for me to take a chair across from him. As I take my recorder out of my case and set it up on the coffee table, Mr. Roth watches me with a wary, unfriendly expression. He's a short, wiry man with a gray buzz cut and a square jaw and he wears loose gray slacks cinched with a thin black belt, and a white shirt open at the collar. A bulky black eyeglass case bulges in his shirt pocket. As I turn on the tape recorder— before I can say anything—Ashley Roth starts speaking.

(Since my initials and Ashley Roth's are the same, to avoid confusion I will go by ME *in this interview.)*

AR: *(Leaning forward.)* Let's get something straight right now. I'm talking to you for one reason, and one reason only: I'm going to make sure you don't lie about my part in this story. I've talked to Tom Lourdes and he said you had the notes from when he interviewed me years ago and that you were likely to construct any kind of fantasy from them. So understand, you're going to use every word I say today, and if you don't I'll sue your ass from here to San Diego. Here. *(He pulls a document of some sort out from under a magazine on the coffee table.)* You're going to sign this, or we don't talk. That's all right, go ahead and look it over. It says you have to use all my interview. My lawyer drew it up. Everything's in order. *(He points a finger at me.)* I'm not one of these old women you've been going around bullying. Tom told me about that, too. But you're not going to pull any tricks here. No sir.

ME: *(I quickly read the document and it seems harmless enough, so I sign it, push it back across the coffee table, and smile.)* Mr. Roth, this kind of confrontation really isn't necessary.

AR: Don't like it, do you? Well, by God, you haven't heard anything yet. First off, I don't like the fact that you got one of those goddamn NEA grants. That's my tax money, by God, and now they're giving it to people for any kind of damn silliness, like pissing in a Mason jar. We fought World War Two on a six-percent income tax and now these whining sons-of-bitches can't get by on any less than twenty. This country . . . *(He waves his hand in front of his face, once, as if knocking away a bee.)* You know, I know some people don't like the Mexicans but I'm glad they're coming up here like a plague of locusts. *They're* not afraid to work. But by God, pretty soon it'll be more than Mexicans. We're going to be kissing Chinese ass before we know it. *(He stops speaking, but keeps me fixed with an angry stare for a moment. Then he sits back, looks down, and brushes at something on the knee of his trouser leg.)*

ME: Well, all right, Mr. Roth. I guess we should get on to our business. The first thing I wanted to ask you, was if you were aware that Howard Hughes knew you had him under surveillance in Reno, and that, in turn, *he* was actually having *you* watched?

AR: *(His head snaps up.)* What?

ME: Hughes was having you watched in Reno.

AR: Bullshit.

170

ME: No, sir, it's true. *(I reach into my case and pull out one of Hughes's diaries. It's roughly the size of a paperback Bible and has a worn brown leather cover. I unbuckle the strap that seals it and open it to the entry I have marked.)* This is dated October eleventh, nineteen-forty-four, and in the heading Hughes has written Reno. About halfway through the entry, he writes, "This man is a waste of our government's tax dollars, but I feel sorry for him because mere laziness couldn't produce such poor performance, it's obviously a lack of native ability. Although I am upset my man following him did not take any and all steps to prevent him from entering our rooms, I will use my influence to make sure he does not get in trouble for fumbling away his pistol. Sometimes, when dealing with incompetents, justice must be tempered with mercy. I suppose most worthwhile men are gone to the military draft, so the FBI is scraping the bottom of the barrel." *(I stop reading and look up at Ashley Roth, who is staring at me with a furious, tight-lipped expression.)*

AR: You son of a bitch.

ME: I know hearing Hughes's opinion of your job performance must be upsetting, and I apologize for having to bring it up. But I'd still like to get your reaction. Did you have any idea he was having you followed?

AR: *(His voice rising.)* That's not Hughes's diary.

ME: Yes, it is. *(I hold up the diary so he can see the pages.)* I don't know if you recognize it or not, but this is Hughes's handwriting.

AR: Where'd you get that?

(I don't answer.)

AR: If it *is* real, *you're* not supposed to have it.

(*I still don't answer.*)

AR: Let me see that thing.

(*He leans across the coffee table and grabs the diary and tries to wrench it from my grip. A tug-of-war ensues, the diary held between our outstretched arms over the coffee table—despite his age, he's surprisingly strong. The sounds of our struggle—mostly his grunts and low curses—fill the tape for twenty seconds, but finally he lets go of the diary and falls back into the couch. He glares at me as he catches his breath.*)

ME: Mr. Roth, really, this all happened years ago, so there's no reason to—

AR: You son of a bitch, you're not going to crucify me like this.

(*With a quickness and agility that surprise me he grabs the baseball bat leaning at his side and with two hands raises it over his head like an ax; he's staring down at my recorder.*)

ME: No!

(*He swings the bat down and smashes the recorder. Plastic shards fly everywhere. Luckily, the blow lands on the speaker and not the tape compartment, and before he can swing again I grab the recorder and jump up from my chair, pick up my case, and leave.*)

Richard Vachaas, pilot and engineer at Hughes Aircraft, 1942–1946, reconstructed from Tom Lourdes's story notes

Late January 1945 I arrived in Vegas in relief of some fellows who'd been stepping and fetching for Hughes—that was going to be my job now. Hughes wasn't there, though, and I had to wait around at a hotel for several days. Finally he showed up. I didn't think he looked too healthy. His color wasn't good, and he wouldn't talk much, but when he did, he spoke so low you could barely understand him. He asked me if I had a partner and I said they'd sent just me. He gave me instructions about handling this box he had. Then he said we were going to Shreveport and for me to file the flight plan. The next day, we left after breakfast with him flying. The first hour he checked me out on the Sikorsky, then he talked about his box. It was in the cabin with us, in the storage area behind the seats with a blackout curtain draped over it. I asked him what was in it.

"You can't know that," he said, "not now, not ever. The one most vital and important instruction I will ever give you is this: never, ever, for any reason, try to find out what is in that box."

Then he said Napoleon had had a strong box where he kept the maps he used to plan his campaigns and that he kept two guards on it twenty-four hours a day. He said Charlemagne had a box built entirely of gold where he kept his Bible and his collection of miniature gold birds. He said the Ark of the Covenant was a box. He said we begin in boxes, which was what a crib was, and that we end in boxes, which was what a coffin was. He said he was sure boxes were one of mankind's original creations, since he could think of no naturally occurring boxes. He kept going on and on, talking about boxes. After a while I stopped listening.

Over Dallas we got a radio message there was a bad thunderstorm up ahead and that we should detour around it. After getting the message Hughes flew about ten minutes without changing course, but from the location of the storm I knew he better change soon.

"You want me to plot a new route?" I said.

"No," he said.

"We really need to," I said.

"I'm flying the plane," he said.

"Yessir, I know. But we need to change course," I said.

He didn't answer. I sat there and tried to think of what to do or say to change his mind—then we caught some wind from the outer edge of the storm and the plane bounced. After Hughes had us back level he nodded over his shoulder. "Do you really want to know what's in that box?" he said.

"Right now, it's not the first thing on my mind," I said.

Another gust of wind rocked the plane and Hughes wrestled with the stick. A dark wall of rain appeared on the horizon.

"We've *got* to get out of this," I said.

"You spend your whole damn life afraid of dying," Hughes said. He opened up the throttle and the plane sped up. Blue lightning flashed ahead of us. "That's really too bad."

Hughes diary entry, February 3, 1945
My plans have been foiled by His whims at every turn so I thought let Him hit me, He's never knocked me down with lightning before. Usually He uses a blonde.

Richard Vachaas, reconstructed from Tom Lourdes's story notes
I told him I was taking the wheel and getting us out of there. He shook his head and said, "It's too late. Our best chance now is to go straight through."

He was right. And truth is, I'd never flown in a storm as bad as that one so I probably couldn't have gotten us out of it anyway.

The lightning was so close the electricity in the air raised the hair on my arms. The sky was pitch-black and the rain was thick and the wind never let up—the wind seemed like it had a mind of its own, like it was bullying us. We were just a toy up there.

In the middle of the storm Hughes was practically standing up to wrestle with the stick, but he started talking about his box again, shouting above the roar of the engines and the rain and wind and thunder. "What is in that box back there," he shouted, "is unexplainable. If I were to tell you what was in it, you would know its physical contents, but that's all. You wouldn't know the truth."

"Please, just get us through this," I said.

"We'll either get through it or we won't," he said, "and it probably doesn't have a helluva lot to do with me. I'm just flying the plane. I'm just the pilot. I can push some pedals and pull the stick, but what's that compared to all the physics working against us? Really, the fact that any airplane stays airborne five seconds in even perfect weather is a miracle. You're an engineer. You know that."

I didn't answer him. I just closed my eyes to pray. The plane was jerking violently and even as heavy as that box was, it was sliding around behind us, thumping from one side of the fuselage to the other. I finally quit praying and opened my eyes and looked at Hughes. He was sitting down now. He had his fedora tipped back on his head and an opened bottle of milk was between his legs. It was sloshing onto his lap but he didn't seem to care. From the expression on his face you would've thought he was driving a car down the street on Sunday morning, but that stick was whipping around in his hands like a snake.

"What's in that box," he said, "is as close as you'll ever get to having the whole ball of yarn in your hands. The alpha and the omega. That's why it's vitally important you follow my instructions regarding it to the letter."

I closed my eyes again and started muttering the Our Father; I was sure I was going to die. Then I felt the bottom fall out and the plane plunged and banked. I opened my eyes and instinctively grabbed my stick. Hughes was no longer holding his. He was staring at his hands, which were shaking violently. I managed to keep us from going into a roll or a stall and got us back level but in that kind of wind I didn't know how long I could keep us there. Hughes was holding his hands together to keep them from shaking.

"Give me some help!" I shouted.

He tried to. He unclasped his hands but as soon as he did they started shaking so much he couldn't hold on to anything.

"I can't," he said.

So I kept flying, and he talked me through it. It was a good thing, too, because I wouldn't have been able to do it without him. It was rough for another ten, fifteen minutes, but we finally came out on the other side of the storm and almost as soon as we did it was time to start our descent toward Shreveport. Hughes said, "Don't you tell anyone what just happened. There are people who would love to have that information and use it against me, so this is very important. Do you understand? You tell anyone and I find out about it, you'll have a price to pay, trust me."

That ticked me off. I didn't like being threatened, plus it was his stupidity that had just put us through such a dangerous experience, so I wasn't in a mood to let his comment, which sounded half-baked to me, just pass off.

"Who'd like to have it?" I said.

"A lot of people," he said. "They're looking for any crack in my armor."

"You just got the shakes," I said. "That's no crime."

"When you've got as much money as I do," he said, "there's no one you can trust. Say I go to a doctor about something simple, a headache or some dizziness. Two days later I might find myself in a straitjacket and someone in my business organization who I never suspected of disloyalty suddenly has power of attorney over my affairs."

"Is that really likely?" I said.

"Yes," he said.

"I don't see how—"

"Just fly the plane," he said.

After we landed, we took a taxi to a hotel near the bus station. I went through setting up that box in its room for the first time— what a damn silly operation that was. That night as I lay in bed I decided I was never getting in a plane with Hughes again. If I lost my job, I lost it.

The next morning, Hughes wasn't in his room. I waited around that day and the next and he didn't show up. I thought about calling the plant, but then decided to wait. I realized I was getting paid to loaf around, which was fine with me.

Luther Tees, Shreveport police officer, 1932–1957, reconstructed from Tom Lourdes's story notes

I was on patrol around midnight when I saw a man sitting on

the curb under a streetlight. He had a quart bottle of milk and a loaf of bread. He was dressed like a bum and he was writing in a notebook he had on the sidewalk beside him. I thought he might be an escapee from the prisoner-of-war camp just outside town—they had a thousand Germans out there they used in the cotton and sugar cane. So I stopped the car and got out and asked him for some identification. He didn't say a word, he didn't look at me, he just kept drawing in his notebook. The light wasn't the best but it looked like he was working on something to do with an airplane. The fact he wouldn't talk made me think, yeah, this probably is a German—he didn't want me to hear his voice.

"I said I need to see some ID," I told him.

He stopped drawing, took a big gulp of milk, a bite of bread, then sat there chewing, looking straight ahead like I wasn't even there.

"Tell me your name," I said sternly.

He didn't answer and his eyes didn't register anything.

"If you don't tell me I'm going to have to arrest you," I said.

He gave me a dirty look then, but he still didn't answer. He went back to drawing.

I went to the car and radioed for help and a few minutes later another car arrived. He didn't give us any trouble when we got him up off the curb. I noticed he walked with a limp, like one leg was shorter than the other. He didn't say one word until we had him at the city jail and then, finally, after I'd banged the blackjack on the table in front of him a couple of times, he said his name was Howard Hughes. I had to smile. I figured he was just another poor soul who'd lost his head and that I'd be calling the state hospital that night. The only problem was the paperwork for that kind of thing was a pisser. I'd be half the night doing it. But if I could get him to tell me some kind of sane-sounding lie I could put in a report, I wouldn't have to send him to Baton Rouge. Of course, I could've made up the lie myself, but I never did like doing that. It was a line I just didn't like to cross.

"I guess you mean *the* Howard Hughes?" I said.

He nodded. "The aviator," he said.

"Look, friend, if you can tell me who you really are I might be able to let you go," I said. "Otherwise I've got to keep you for vagrancy."

"I'm not a vagrant," he said. Then he slipped out of one of his tennis shoes and in the bottom of it was an inch-high stack of money—there was his limp. I got the money out. It was all hundreds. Son of a bitch, I said to myself, I might have a hold-up man on my hands, and one that wasn't too smart, either, showing me the money like that. I handcuffed him to his chair. Then I picked up his notebook and started looking through it. Lots of real precise sketches, like something a professional would do. I held up one of them and asked him what it was.

"That's the tail section of a reconnaissance plane I'm building for the military," he said.

"Look, I'm tired of fooling with you. Tell me who you really are," I said.

"I'm Howard Hughes," he said.

So I put him in the drunk tank. I figured if nice wouldn't work, maybe that would. Right away he started yelling he wanted his notebook, but I kept it and looked through it, thinking he would've written his name in it somewhere. The pages were filled with math equations and drawings, and the only thing not like that was a page where he'd written in big letters, I AM NOT AFRAID.

Since the notebook didn't have anything useful I went down there and gave it back to him to shut him up. He was the only one in the cell awake. The other three were passed out. Stank like a son of a bitch in there because one of the drunks had messed himself both ways.

"What's all that math about?" I asked.

"Airplanes," he said.

"Well, it makes you out to be an educated man," I said.

"I told you, I'm Howard Hughes."

"Then why're you going around like a hobo?" I asked.

He plopped down right where he was and sat Indian-style on the floor and started thumbing through the notebook. I squatted so we were face-to-face. "Come on, tell me. Why is Howard Hughes going around like this?"

He kept staring at the notebook, turning pages. "At least one thing in life must make sense," he said. "Now, these do make *some* sense," and he pointed to some figures in his notebook, "but these aren't much more than the kinds of little disturbances a fly might leave in a pile of loose shit."

I watched him a moment. "Say," I said. "You didn't maybe lose someone overseas, did you?"

"No. But Ava Gardner won't marry me," he said.

I shook my head and stood up. It looked like I was going to be doing that paperwork after all. "Well, you're still young," I said. "Maybe she'll change her mind yet."

"That's one lie I've stopped believing," he said.

I decided to give it one last shot. "Look," I said, "I know how it is. I got a boy overseas right now and sometimes I think I can't take it. But when I get too worried about that or anything else I think about deep-sea fishing, and I manage to go to Florida every year and fish for a week. Down to the Keys if I can. You just got to keep your mind on something like that. So whatever's bothering you, just—"

"I won an air race in Florida in thirty-two," he said.

"Just tell me who you are," I said, "and where you got that stack of money. Then I can let you go."

He looked up from his notebook, but he wasn't looking at me. "Florida," he said.

"That's where you got the money?" I said.

"Florida could be Nevada," he said.

"What'd you mean?" I said.

He shut the notebook and stood up. "Call the Blue Chateau Hotel and ask for Richard Vachaas," he said. "He'll confirm that I'm Howard Hughes."

Hughes diary entry, February 8, 1945

Reasons Florida Will Work

1. Relatively undeveloped, though not quite as good in this respect as Nevada.
2. Warm climate, allowing year-round golf.
3. Governor Ellis is a drinker.

4. Easy access to ports and to the oilfields of Texas and Central America.

5. Short air routes to the East Coast cities and Europe.

6. If you don't like golf, you can try ocean sports.

7. Moving east will get me away from actresses once and for all.

Let the gangsters have Nevada. Of course, there will be a honeymoon when the public flocks to the poker palaces and cheap whores but I have to believe eventually the American people will tire of these things and will learn that games of chance are heavily fixed in favor of those running them, anybody who has been to a carnival and thrown a baseball at a stack of milk bottles knows there is little to no chance of winning. But if they are that stupid, if they keep going to gambling houses full of diseased whores to hand their hard-earned money to greasy idiots who don't know how to do anything except buy a gross of dice and playing cards and lay some green felt across fifty kitchen tables and call the whole thing a casino, then screw them.

Hughes diary entry, August 6, 1945
If Walt Disney shaved off the left and right sides of his moustache and left only the part under his nose he'd look like Hitler except the German had a better dye job. I can understand losing Nevada to the false hope gambling gives and also the drinking and easy sex, but losing Florida to a damn cartoonist is more than I can take. Disney is in the land-buying stage for building Coney Island type parks in both California and Florida. He calls the parks imitations of cities, only cities where no one has to work.

They will have fake main streets and boardwalk rides and robots that look like figures in a wax museum but that can move and talk and sing. Disney says the parks will be dreams given a steel and concrete existence. I asked him if he was putting any churches in his fake cities. No, people don't want to think about that on vacation he said. How about a fake hospital with a robot that looks like a man who just had a leg amputated? That happens most days in any city you pick I said. Or how about a robot screaming during childbirth? Or a fake poultry processing plant with thousands of fake dead headless chickens hanging upside down with fake blood running out their necks into a gutter and then a pit? People could throw coins into the pit of fake blood and make wishes, then go have a nice chicken dinner in one of your restaurants. By that point he was looking at me with a dull glazed look that was equaled in stupidity by the semi-conscious besotted smile of the governor. I asked the governor if he was left handed. He looked confused for a second, then said, no, right. I said I was surprised, I figured he wrote left handed since I'd never seen him without a highball glass in his right.

Florida goes to Disney. He gets the tax exemptions, the guarantees for the electricity and water he needs. The way things stand now I couldn't get a permit for a hot dog stand in this state.

They dropped an atom bomb on the Japs today.

Article titled "Howard Hughes Returns" from the society page of the November, 2, 1945, issue of the New York Post
After a long, long time away, Howard Hughes has been spotted all over town recently wearing black tie and tails and, egads,

tennis shoes. Mr. Hughes puts the lie to the old adage that the clothes make the man; apparently, the man makes the clothes.

Mr. Hughes came sailing into town in October, from no one knows where, in the world's fifth largest yacht, which he recently bought and rechristened *The Gloria*. Could this be in honor of a certain Miss G. Vanderbilt who has had such a successful coming-out season? Recently this reporter spotted Miss Vanderbilt and Mr. Hughes at 21, and May and December seemed to be getting along famously. However, later the same week, outside a Manhattan nightclub, Mr. Hughes was seen entering a cab with another striking deb, a Miss B. Hutton.

What will his yacht be called next week?

Painters, stay at the ready.

Alton Reece's second interview with Tom Lourdes

At the Tremelo Retirement Home I unload the box from my wagon and wheel it to the entrance. As I'm struggling to get it through the front door, a well-dressed man and woman approach from inside and ask what I'm doing. I back the box out of the doorway and they step outside, where I introduce myself and tell them I have an appointment with Tom Lourdes. The man says they know who I am, they're the home's comanagers and they've been waiting for me, but appointment or not, I'm not bringing a coffin inside. I explain the box isn't a coffin and tell them to check my story with Tom Lourdes—he knows about Hughes's box and I'm certain he'll want me to bring this in for him to see. The man nods to the woman and she disappears into the building, leaving the man and me facing each other with nothing to say. He's heavyset, bald, wearing a black suit, and his forehead and upper lip are covered with a sheen of perspiration. Then a van bus pulls up and starts letting out elderly women; I wheel the box off the sidewalk to get out of their way, and as they approach the entrance they all stare at the box, some with alarm. As the manager holds the door open for them he makes apologies about the box and explains it isn't *a coffin. Then the woman manager returns and with obvious disappointment says Mr. Lourdes apparently does want to see the box.*

In the dayroom where we did our first interview, Tom Lourdes sits in his wheelchair wearing a new-looking, dark green, shiny silk bathrobe. His yellowish-white hair is slicked down and neatly parted to one side. Susan, the attendant I met on my first visit, sits next to him—she gives me a quick smile. However, as soon as I enter the room Tom Lourdes fixes me with a withering stare. He has a cushioned writing desk in his lap and on top of it are copies of the stories I built from his notes, the pages filled with scratchings and margin notes in red ink. Three chairs are arranged in a semicircle in front of Mr. Lourdes and Susan, so I place the box between that semicircle and them, and then the two managers and I sit down, with me in the middle chair.

TL: Where's your recorder?

AR: *(I produce my micro-recorder from my shirt pocket.)* This has been running since I entered the room. It's digital, state of the art. Picks up anything within—

TL: Your gizmo doesn't interest me.

AR: *(I sigh.)* Of course not.

MALE MANAGER: *(Sternly.)* Mr. Reece, there's some things I want you to understand.

AR: *(Forcing a smile.)* Yes?

MALE MANAGER: Sheila and I are sitting in on this interview at

Tom's request, but even if he hadn't asked us I'm sure we'd be here anyway. You see, two weeks ago we were contacted by a private investigator about a matter concerning you.

FEMALE MANAGER: *(About fifty, plump, leaning forward to look around me at her partner.)* We agreed not bring that up, didn't we? *(She smiles stiffly.)* We're not getting involved in that matter. We're here for Tom today, and that's all.

MALE MANAGER: *(Impatiently.)* I'm *not* going to be an accessory to a crime.

FEMALE MANAGER: Carl, please.

MALE MANAGER: I told the investigator you were going to be here today, Mr. Reece.

FEMALE MANAGER: *(Exasperated, dropping her prim demeanor.)* Oh good Lord.

AR: No, that's fine. I hope he does show up so we can settle this, whatever it is. I'd appreciate knowing, though, just what—

TL: *(Interrupting.)* All these shenanigans . . . *(He shakes his head.)* And this silly box. God, you don't care about Hughes. You don't have any real feeling for the man. It takes more than dragging this thing around to understand him.

AR: Mr. Lourdes, I'm sorry you feel that way. *(A pause, and then with building emotion.)* But if that's really how you see what I'm doing, then you don't know what love is.

TL: What? Did you say *love*? *(He picks up a paper-clipped story from his lap and waves it.)* I've spent *weeks* trying to clean up this mess you sent me. *(He lowers the story and clumsily thumbs through it.)* These are *all* lies. Time and again you take one or two insignificant details from my notes and concoct whole fictions from them. This one here . . . *(He shakes the story at me.)* The stories you put in Brucks Randall's mouth are almost *complete* falsehoods. But the worst of it is that you portray Hughes as some kind of . . . I don't know what. *(He pauses, and as he looks at me his eyes narrow.)* No, that's not right. I do know what you're doing. I know *exactly* what you're doing. You're making Hughes into the man you wish *you* yourself were. It's an adolescent fantasy of a great man, nothing but unspeakable exploits with women and daredevil adventures. A pornographic cartoon. A sexual epic filled with meaningless stunts. *(He stops. His face is red and his breathing is rapid and shallow. A string of spittle hangs at one corner of his mouth; Susan hands him a tissue and he wipes it away.)*

FEMALE MANAGER: Susan, bring the machine over and check Tom's blood pressure.

MALE MANAGER: *(Glaring at me.)* I hope you're happy.

SUSAN: *(In one quick motion she stands up and snaps her head toward the male manager.)* This isn't Alton's fault.

(A short silence)

FEMALE MANAGER: *(Nodding toward me.)* Susan, do you know him?

(Susan won't look at her. She crosses the room to the vital-signs machine, six feet tall with a variety of cords and digital gauges.)

AR: I'll answer that. When I found out Mr. Lourdes was on some kind of crusade against me, calling people all over the country, I phoned Susan to see if she could tell me what was going on. We developed an acquaintance.

FEMALE MANAGER: *(Lilting.)* I see.

(Susan fits the cuff on Tom Lourdes's bicep, pushes a button, the machine hums and the cuff inflates.)

TL: *(His voice low and tired.)* The box Hughes carried. Not this one, of course . . . *(He pauses for breath, and before he can continue the machine beeps, signaling it has finished its reading. The red digital numbers say 161/103. Everyone except Tom Lourdes is looking at them.)*

TL: This box, you make too much of it. *(Pause for breath.)* I'm certain Hughes saw it as an elaborate joke on the press and the FBI. It meant nothing to him. *(Another pause.)* It was a red herring.

AR: How do you know?

TL: I knew him. I understand him.

(My cell phone starts ringing.)

AR: *(Exasperated.)* Good Lord. *(I open the phone and answer.)* Carol, hi, I'm in the middle of something . . . Well, they *better* pay it. Expenses are covered, that's in the contract, and I expect— *(She interrupts, and while I'm listening, a very tall man enters the room. He's at least six nine, with arms and legs that are long, thin, and loose-looking like a puppet's. His khakis are two inches too short for him and his brown socks are bunched around his ankles. The male manager stands and greets him and they move to a corner and begin whispering.)* All right, look, I've got to go. We'll talk about this later. *(I hang up.)*

MALE MANAGER: *(Approaching my chair.)* This is Mr. Yeary, the private investigator I told you about.

YEARY: *(For a moment he stands over the box and looks down at it. There's complete silence in the room, except for Tom Lourdes's labored breathing. Then Yeary looks up at me and smiles, revealing very gray teeth.)* Mr. Reece, my client is concerned about a ring that's in your possession.

AR: Yes, well, I've got—

YEARY: *(Interrupting, holding up a hand.)* Look, I know you have a release for it, and that's not what's at question. What isn't entirely clear is whether Lisa Trundle had the right to give that release.

AR: Well, I made the agreement in good faith and, well, the terms of it haven't been broken on my part.

YEARY: Yes, we understand this is a murky situation legally and my client wants to settle this without a lot of fuss, so—*(He smiles broadly.)*—if I could just have evidence that you're still in possession of the ring, that you haven't sold it, then my client would be satisfied.

AR: *(Sighing.)* Well, I'll have to go out to the car and get it.

YEARY: That's fine.

(I get up and leave the room, walk outside and get in the station wagon, then start the engine and drive away.)

The Double

In the summer of 1947, Hughes was subpoenaed to testify at Senate hearings on war racketeering. The allegations against him were that he had received $40 million in government contracts for various projects, including the "Spruce Goose," and hadn't delivered anything, and that he had paid bribes to military officials, including a colonel who was the late FDR's son. There was little truth to these charges. Hughes's projects were on schedule, and although he *had* wined and dined and provided call girls for FDR's son and many others, so had every other defense contractor of any size. The real motivation for Hughes's subpoena was that Pan American Airways wanted the overseas air routes that Hughes's newly acquired airline, TWA, had just won. The chairman of the committee conducting the hearings, Senator Owen Brewster, was in the pocket of Pan American and before the subpoena was issued Brewster phoned Hughes and told him he would be left alone if he sold the routes to Pan American. Hughes let Brewster finish, then asked him which side of his ass he would like to kiss, the left or the right.

The subpoena for Hughes was never served. U.S. marshals scoured the country but never found him. Hughes avoided the marshals through use of a double. A Hughes aide accidentally discovered an almost exact double for Hughes in, of all places, Schwab's Drugstore in Hollywood, a place legendary for the "discovery" of unknown actors and actresses. The man, Brucks Randall, was an actor having difficulty getting work exactly because he looked so much like Howard Hughes. Randall was given lessons in talking and acting like Hughes, was dressed in a typical Hughes wardrobe, and then was sent to various locations in the west to stage fake Hughes sightings. The marshals were always a step too late to catch him and during the whole two-month period the double was used, Hughes was hiding out in a suburban Los Angeles home purchased under a false name.

In most doppelgänger stories—*Dr. Jekyll and Mr. Hyde* is a well-known example—the double, or alternate personality of the protagonist, represents our inappropriate desires. Sin is what doppelgänger stories are about. However, instead of having a "bad" double, Hughes tried to create a good one. In a series of memos sent to Brucks Randall over the two months of his employment, Hughes instructed him "to do some of the things I can't seem to bring myself to do, for whatever damn reason." Randall was paid four hundred dollars a week—a fine salary at the time—plus expenses.

Hughes memo to Brucks Randall, dated June 2, 1947

1. Dress in disguise so I don't look like me. Use a fake beard, a bowler, a cane, a built-up left shoe. Walk with a limp. When I speak, use a British accent. My name is Henry Vontobel.

2. Go to the morning service at the 3rd Street Methodist Church.

3. If anyone asks what happened to my leg, say I was an RAF fighter pilot during the war and was injured when I had to bail out over the Channel. If anyone asks what I'm doing in America, tell them I married an American girl who was a Red Cross volunteer in London. Her name is Janice. She is visiting her sister in Cleveland. We have just moved to Tucson and I am seeking work as a salesman.

4. When the offering is taken, put the supplied envelope in the plate. Do not keep the envelope and say to yourself, as I might: To hell with these self-righteous jackasses, they're not getting a dime of my money to spend on a new Buick so the minister can drive his mouthy wife to bridge parties. Remember, I am Henry Vontobel, British war hero, grateful to be alive and looking forward to starting a family and a new life in America. My wife is a knockout and a sweet girl too. All the death and suffering

191

I saw during the war and all the ignorance and pettiness and blackhearted intentions I see around me daily have some ultimate meaning even if I don't know what it is.

5. When the congregation prays, bow my head and close my eyes. Do not look around to see how everyone looks while they are praying.

6. After the service, shake hands with confidence. I have no fear of infection.

7. There is a good chance, given my status as a war hero and a newcomer, that I will be invited to dinner after the service. Accept. Eat with gusto whatever they serve no matter how filthy or imperfectly prepared, participate in the conversation no matter how trite, play with the children afterward and tell them stories about my wartime flying exploits, though say nothing that would unman their father. Chances are he does not have the tales of derring-do to tell that I do. If anyone asks my age, say thirty-one.

8. Never let me be caught alone with the wife or any daughter older than 16. Do not try to charm the women; they will be enamored of me enough as it is. I must guard against the inclination to arrange a meeting with one of them for later in the week. If one does make a flirtatious move, act like it didn't happen. But be careful. They are tricky. There is always a smokescreen. I might find myself alone with the wife or older daughter in the kitchen, maybe I have limped in to refill my coffee cup and she is doing the dishes, and she might ask a little too brightly and eagerly when my wife will be back in town, she'd love to meet her—generally this is done so she can

know how long the coast is clear. Don't give a definite date. She might ask what hotel I am staying in: tell her I am changing hotels tomorrow, and I'm not sure where I'm going.

9. If something does happen with the wife or an older good-looking daughter, a hurried embrace in the kitchen or maybe a longer encounter in the cellar or sewing room or some such place where I have gone to see some woman's project of hers she wants to show off—her canned goods, the newest model wringer washer, a half-finished quilt— do not obsess about her for days and weeks. Think about her for the rest of the night, then let her go! No meetings later in the week.

10. If I do have a minor slip with one of the women, a goof up that Sunday or later in the week while her husband or father is at work, I must immediately upon parting from her get on my knees and ask for forgiveness instead of trying to figure out a way to meet some of her friends. Think about my lovely wife whom I've betrayed. Suffer, and let my suffering instruct me.

Brucks Randall, reconstructed from Tom Lourdes's story notes
Hughes said go to church in Tucson in disguise as a Brit. It was one of those churches where everybody's smile looked like it was held up with safety pins, so after the service I got plenty of lunch invitations. I accepted the choir director's because he had a daughter who looked good enough to make a deacon punch out a stained glass window. She was a college girl and during the afternoon I set up a lunch date with her—I said I

193

wanted her to give me the lowdown on Tucson since I was new to town. On Tuesday we met, one thing led to another, and she came back to my hotel. Hughes had said don't touch the women, but I did and the sky didn't fall, so I had her over again on Friday.

Saturday morning a knock on my door woke me up. Two men were there and they pushed their way into the room and put tape over my mouth and then beat hell out of me, only they didn't touch my face, it was gut and kidney punches and blackjack work on my legs. Then they sat me up on the bed and stood in front of me, Frick and Frack in black suits. They were the same size. Big and square. Put a nickel in their ear a Coca-Cola would pop out their ass. One of them yanked the tape off my mouth, which left me about enough moustache to pass for fourteen.

"Mr. Hughes has to do better," he said. "He has to learn to leave the women alone and be faithful to his wife, or this will happen again. This will happen every time Mr. Hughes is unfaithful."

"What?" I said.

"That's what I'm supposed to tell you," he said. Then the other one pulled five one-hundred-dollar bills from his inside jacket pocket and threw them on the bed. "You get this for taking the beating," the talker said, "but I'm supposed to tell you this is the last time you'll get paid for taking one. Mr. Hughes has to start learning from his mistakes."

"This is nuts," I said.

The talker just shrugged. They left.

I probably would've quit but those were tough times. I wasn't finding work as an actor, mostly because I looked exactly like Hughes, and straight jobs were scarce, too, with so many veterans back looking for work. If I'd had a pot to piss in I would've taken that five hundred and run. But I wanted to build up a better stake. I wanted enough to start a little grocery in my hometown in Wyoming.

Hughes memo to Brucks Randall, dated June 29, 1947

1. Go to Las Vegas.

2. Read Jeremiah and Isaiah.

3. I have phoned Bugsy Siegel and arranged a meeting with him at the construction site where his casino is being built. Wear the gray suit, shoulder holster, pistol, and navy overcoat. A person like me will not be checked for weapons; that's just in movies. Shine my shoes. I will go with two of the Mormons, who will report back to me my actions during the meeting so I can be certain I have carried out my wishes.

4. After walking in I say:

"I'm not going to let you ruin this country, Siegel."

He will probably be sitting behind a big desk with gunmen spaced out around the room—he doesn't have the guts to face me alone, man to man. Sweep my finger around the room and say, "Afraid to talk to me without your girlfriends?"

5. The two Mormons will be terrified. Notice their terror, but stand fast.

6. Siegel will scowl at me silently. I say, "I'm tired of

wasting my time. Let me speak to the pants of this outfit. Where is she?"

7. He'll say, "What do you want?"

8. I say:

"You will sell me this property we're standing on right now, Siegel, and get the hell out of Nevada, or you're going to wish your mother was picking apples the day she decided to open her legs for the three or four sons of bitches who could be your father. I'm not going to let you turn this country into a bunch of lazy bastards who think they can turn five dollars into ten by watching a roulette wheel spin and drinking watered-down liquor at the same time. It's just not going to happen. We didn't just fight a war so you can turn this country into something like France."

"France?" he might say.

"France," I'll say. "Think about it and you might understand. If too much of your brain isn't currently occupied with the strain of keeping your hands out of your pants."

9. Before I am finished he will probably be motioning for the gunmen to move in. I jerk the pistol out and lean over the desk and hold it a foot from his forehead. "Everyone stop where they stand," I say. The room freezes. "Everyone get in the corner of the room to the left of this desk," I say. They do. I tell the Mormons to take their guns.

10. Siegel says, "Hughes, you're a dead man."

11. I say, "Probably."

12. I take an extra gun from the trembling hand of one of the Mormons. I say, "One last chance, Siegel. Will you sell out to me?"

13. He says, "Kiss my ass, Hughes. Kill me, somebody else'll be here tomorrow."

14. I say, "Let's hope his name isn't Bugsy."

15. I save America.

16. I have guilt. But I think of the children who will eat because money has not been lost gambling, the wives who will not be beaten, the non-gamblers whose lives will not be less than they could have been because the empty values fostered by gambling will not permeate the country. I will probably never feel completely good about what I have done, but I did what I thought was best for the country and if I'm wrong I'll find out someday. I'll bear the consequences of my actions if I have to. But at least I acted with the courage I couldn't muster before.

17. I should say my lines exactly as they are written. I should not ad lib. Every actor thinks he is a director and vice-versa. I should not fall into that trap.

Brucks Randall, reconstructed from Tom Lourdes's story notes

In Vegas the guy who took the instructions off the phone walked into my room and sat down on the edge of the bed. I was lying there smoking. He was a Mormon but he got one of my cigarettes and lit it. He said, "We've got to do something."

"What is it?" I said. He handed me the instructions and I read them.

"Of course, we can't do what he wants," he said, "but we've

got to show up for the meeting. If we at least show up, we might keep our jobs."

"Your problem, not mine," I said. "I'm not doing it. I'm quitting."

"All you've got to do is wish Siegel luck," he said. "I'll give you an extra fifty."

I told him no.

"Seventy-five," he said.

"It sounds like Siegel and Hughes are having a piss fight," I said, "and I'm not getting in the middle of it."

"I'll give you an extra hundred," he said. "Look, nothing'll happen. Siegel doesn't want trouble, and doing something to Howard Hughes in the middle of the day on a construction site would be trouble."

I hadn't thought about it that way. He was right, so I said I'd do it for an extra hundred.

The meeting was nothing. Siegel was going over blueprints with an architect when we walked in, and he hardly paid us any attention. A couple of muscle guys were standing around. I kept my hat pulled down low over my eyes and wished Siegel luck with his casino, said things looked like they were coming along. He looked at me kind of funny, kind of suspicious, then broke out in a smile and said, sure, no hard feelings. I said right, no hard feelings, and left.

That night I woke up and Frick and Frack were sitting in chairs pulled up to my bed, watching me. I about jumped out of my skin. I curled up into a ball and waited for the first punch. The one who hadn't spoken at all during the first visit got up and turned on the bathroom light, then sat down again and started slapping a blackjack against his thigh, *thwap, thwap*. The one who had done all the talking was wearing half-glasses down on his nose and had papers in his lap. They were dressed the same, in dark suits and white shirts open at the collar. The talker switched on a penlight and pointed it at his papers.

"Mr. Hughes is a coward," he read. "He is ashamed of himself. Why didn't he do what he planned today? He let himself and his country down. How does he explain this to himself?" He pointed the penlight in my eyes.

"You want me to answer?" I said.

"I'm just doing what it says," he said.

"Fellows, I'm just like you," I said. "I'm the hired help. I'm getting paid to impersonate Howard Hughes. He wanted me to kill Bugsy Siegel today. Jesus, I couldn't do that."

He pointed the penlight back down at the paper. "Mr. Hughes always has an excuse," he read. Then he nodded to the quiet one, who stopped drumming the blackjack and pulled out a .38 and pointed it at me. The talker handed the penlight to him and he pointed it at the paper for him, then the talker pulled out a .38, too, and held it out to me butt end first and read, "Take this, if you're man enough."

"I don't want it," I said.

"Go on, take it," he read. "Mr. Hughes knows he wants to put himself out of his misery. For a failure like Mr. Hughes, there's no other choice."

"Are you fucking crazy?" I said.

The talker looked up. "Watch your mouth," he said. "I'm just reading this shit."

"I'll give you everything I've got if you'll just let me leave.

I've got almost two thousand. I'll tell you how to get your hands on it if you'll just let me go."

"Two thousand don't even come close," he said. Then he looked at the paper and read, "Take the pistol, you gutless bastard, and finish the job Ava Gardner started."

"I'm not doing it," I said.

He nodded at the quiet one, who pulled back the hammer on the .38.

"How would you rather die," the talker said, "at your own hand or at the hands of your enemies, those who would destroy you and sap your . . ." and he stopped. He stared at the paper. Then he held it up to me and pointed. "What's that?" he asked.

"Vitality," I said.

"And sap your vitality," he said. "At least have that victory. Do not give the bastards that satisfaction. Mr. Hughes has failed in every area of his life and it would be best if he just killed himself so his wealth could get out of his hands and do some good in the world."

"I'm not doing it," I said.

He set the pistol in his lap, shuffled the papers and pulled out a new one. "Good," he read. "Mr. Hughes has made the correct choice. He will live and . . ." he stopped and held up the paper again.

"Wreak vengeance."

"And wreak vengeance on his enemies," he said. "Mr. Hughes cannot be destroyed by the petty . . ." and he held up the paper.

"Functionaries."

"Functionaries who are trying to destroy all he has built."

Then the quiet one pulled out a stack of bills, laid them on the bed, and without another word the two of them stood up and moved their chairs back under the card table and left, closing the door very quietly behind them. I turned on the lamp and counted the money. It was fifty hundreds. Five grand.

Hughes memo to Brucks Randall, dated July 11, 1947

1. I have a suite of rooms reserved at the Beverly Hills Hotel. Get a haircut, but have the barber come to my room. I should not be seen in public yet.

2. I have called Ava and arranged to meet her at 10 p.m. in the Aqua Room. I want to be 45 minutes to 90 minutes late, calling her two or three times to make excuses but also to reassure. If she has to wait she will start drinking—and that is exactly what I want.

3. I dress well.

4. I unscrew the bulb from the rooflight in the car.

5. I whisk into the now-crowded Aqua Room, acknowledge all hellos with a nod, then whisk Ava out to the car. If she wants to argue about my lateness and make a scene I guide her firmly by the arm, a smile fixed on my face for the benefit of onlookers.

6. She never leaves the car unless it is to go to the bathroom, in which case I stop at a filling station. If she wants more booze, I have a half-pint in the glove box.

7. I take her to the cross. If I forget where it is, I have directions in the glove box.

8. I park near the cross. However, we don't get out and stand under the cross and I don't propose marriage or read from the book of vows. I sit in the car with Ava and say:

a) "No matter how I pursue you in the future, no matter what I say to you or do to win you after this night, I will never be the kind of man who makes a good husband and you should always remember that. Protect yourself."

b) "Despite all the other women I have been with, you are the one true love of my life."

c) "I love your spirit, intelligence, and beauty."

d) "My best self would never do anything to hurt you. But for whatever reason, my best self comes and goes more than I would like."

e) "I pray there is an afterlife so my best self can have a small chance of being with you forever. That is the one hope that keeps me trying to be a better man than I've been so far."

f) "The last thing I want to say, Ava, is that I can stomach any of the other men you have been seeing, but if you are ever with Mickey Rooney again I will kill myself."

9. She will be moved. If she tries to kiss or make other advances I say, "I am not worth half of what you have to offer."

10. If this makes her even more ardent, as any kind of reticence often does, I should quickly start the car and drive away.

11. Under no circumstances should I kiss her or touch

her. I want an innocence in this encounter that has not been in any encounter for many years and will probably never be in one again after this night. This night will be a ray of light shining in a dark sea of meaningless squalor and heaving flesh.

12. I repeat: I do not touch her. If I kiss her or touch any part of her body, even if my hand just lightly brushes the hair on her forearm, I will be severely beaten, a beating worse than any I have had so far. If I go so far as to have relations with her in the car, I will be medically castrated at a secret location. I might even be killed, depending on what kind of mood I am in.

Brucks Randall, reconstructed from Tom Lourdes's story notes
I was nervous as hell about Ava Gardner. We met at this nightclub—thank God it was dark and she'd had a few drinks, because I wasn't sure I could fool her. I said I wanted to leave and she got up without a word and walked out with me and got in the car. She asked where we were going.

"This place where there's a cross," I told her. "It's got a good view. I want you to see it." One of the Mormons had told me about the "Hughes" cross. It was on a hill in Hollywood and if Hughes couldn't get a woman to sleep with him, he'd take her up there and stand with her in front of the cross and read from a book of vows and tell her they were now married in the eyes of God so it was okay to go to bed.

"I know all about your cross," she said, "and I don't know why we'd need it at this point. But we'll go there if it makes you happy." Then she opened the glove box and reached for the bottle of whiskey like she knew it was there.

I didn't say anything until we got to the cross—I was too nervous—and she didn't either, she just looked out her window and drank. At the cross I parked on the shoulder and started saying all this stuff Hughes wanted said. As I was talking, she took her shoes off and put her feet up on the dash, then pulled her dress down into her lap and unhooked her garters and started rolling a stocking off.

She said, "It sounds like a scriptwriter wrote this for you."

"No, this is from the heart."

"Have you got a cold?" she said. "You sound like you've got a cold."

"I could be catching one."

"Well, I don't want it."

"I don't think it's contagious," I said.

Twenty minutes later I had her naked. I knew Hughes was probably having us watched, but I didn't care. It was Ava Gardner.

I figured I could disappear that night before Frick and Frack got to me.

So we kept going. But right when I was ready to start in, a light shined into the car. She started cursing. I raised up and then my door swung open and there was the talker from Frick and Frack, dressed like a policeman.

"Get out," he said.

I didn't move so he reached in and grabbed me by the arm and pulled me out.

The quiet one was on the other side of the car and had his

flashlight pointed at Ava. No one spoke for maybe twenty seconds while she got her dress on and I got my pants up from around my ankles. The talker wouldn't let me back in the car for my shirt and shoes.

Ava said, "Do you know who we are?"

"Yes, ma'am," the talker said.

"Are these the people from the government?" she said. "Are they the ones looking for you?"

"No," I said.

"Let me see your badge," she said.

He produced what looked like a real L.A. Sheriff's Department badge and handed it to her.

"We're sorry we had to bother you when we did," he said, "but we have information that parties intent on hurting Mr. Hughes are close by."

"Who?" she said.

"I can't say," he said.

"Ridiculous," she said and handed the badge back. "What's really going on?"

"I'm not Howard Hughes," I blurted out, "I just look like him. He hired me to impersonate him. He ordered me to bring you up here. These two work for him."

She didn't say anything. She just shook her head.

"My name is Brucks Randall," I said, "and I'm sorry about what just happened with us but if you leave right now I'm dead. Hughes said he'd kill me if we did anything."

"Is this one of your loyalty tests, Howard?" she said. "Are you trying to see if I'll act like some foolish girl in a movie and stay by your side?"

"No. I'm telling you the truth. I'm not Hughes."

"Brucks," she said. "That's a cowboy name. It's too outlandish for even you."

"I tell you, I'm not him."

"Oh stop it, for godssake," she said. "Get in. Let's get out of here."

"He has to stay with us for his own safety, ma'am," the talker said, and I felt the cold tip of a pistol push into the small of my back.

"Stop this charade," she said. "It's getting on my nerves."

"He's got a pistol on me right now," I said.

"Oh God. You stop it, too," she said, "or I *will* leave."

"You need to leave right now, ma'am," the talker said.

"Please," I said, "as long as you stay I'm okay. I don't believe Hughes would hurt you."

"That's it," she said and she scooted under the wheel and started the car.

"No," I said.

She didn't say another word. She just pulled out, tires screeching.

After the car disappeared around the first curve going down the hill the quiet one moved up and jerked my arms behind my back and taped my wrists together. He taped my mouth. The talker put on glasses. He had papers again and he pointed his flashlight at them.

"Mr. Hughes has had his chances," he read, "but this was his last one. He could have avoided this if he had just expressed his love to Miss Gardner and left it at that, but no, he had to use this cross, once again, for his own selfish pleasure. Mr. Hughes has committed this blasphemy for the last time. He is one of the proud of the earth, but now his offending member is going to be cut off."

I wheeled and started running down the hill. After a few seconds, I heard heavy breathing behind me and then a fist to the back of the neck dropped me. I rolled down the hill; it was steep and with my hands tied behind my back it took me awhile to stop myself, but when I did and tried to get up again, a foot between my shoulder blades shoved me back down. A pillowcase or hood or something was thrown over my head.

I was led back up the hill and put into the backseat of a car. They taped my ankles together. Then we rode for maybe twenty minutes, and when we stopped, they dragged me out of the car and into a building. I know we went through two doors because I heard them open and shut. I was laid on a bed and my feet and hands were untaped and the hood was removed. They untaped my mouth. Then they left the room. The door closed and the lock clicked. From my fall I had bad road burns on my chest, shoulders and stomach, these raw exposed patches of pink and red flesh. They hurt like hell and had asphalt grime dug into them.

The room was painted white and had a white tile floor—everything was white. Over my bed was a light on a collapsible arm like the ones over a dentist's chair. It was turned off. The bed was iron and painted white, and there were three windows in the room, all in a row on the far wall, the glass in them painted white. A white metal straightback chair sat at the foot of the bed and a white metal hospital-looking dresser was next to the door. There was nothing else in the room, no pictures, nothing.

I was certain I was getting ready to either die or have my balls cut off. I started panicking. I got up and tried the windows but they were locked and I couldn't figure out how. So I took a pillowcase from the bed and put it over my fist and punched at a pane of glass—they were big nine-pane windows—and the glass broke but didn't shatter, and in the cracks between the shards of glass I saw wire mesh. I hit it again, wincing, gritting my teeth—anytime I moved my arms my burns stretched and hurt even worse—and this time some glass fell out but the mesh didn't give. I realized I'd have to break the tic-tac-toe frame that held the panes. I got the chair and swung it into the window. More glass cracked, but the frame stayed intact. I hit the window again and again and eventually broke off enough wood to see that the frame was metal behind a wood veneer.

I quit and laid down. The places where I'd broken the glass let some cool air into the room. I must have laid there for an hour. My burns were drying out and starting to itch and it was driving me crazy. Once I started crying but I stopped. I didn't want to go out that way if I could help it.

Finally the door opened and in walked Hughes himself. He was naked as a jaybird and carrying a white metal case. Son of a bitch really did look like me. It was uncanny. Like looking in a mirror.

He walked to the window, tiptoeing around the broken glass, and examined what I'd done. Then he pulled the straightback chair over beside the bed and sat down. He laid the case on the bed and opened it and inside were medical instruments and supplies. "Are you in pain?" he asked.

I nodded.

He took out a syringe and a dark glass bottle and started drawing its contents into the syringe. "This should help," he said.

"What is it?" I said.

"Just medicine," he said.

He motioned for me to roll onto my side and I did—I thought it possible he was giving me something that would kill me, but my burns were hurting so bad by that time, itching so much, I was ready to risk anything to make it stop. He yanked my pants down off my hip and gave me the shot. I could tell from the way it hit me it had morphine in it. My pain eased right away.

He took gauze, a jar of sulfa, and forceps out of the case. "We've got to get you cleaned up so you don't get infected," he said. He positioned the spotlight over my chest and turned it on. It blinded me and I had to close my eyes. Then I felt the cold forceps in one of my burns, picking at a tiny pebble. He dropped it into a metal pan, *ping*.

"Looks like it's not too easy being me," he said.

I nodded.

"But the pay's pretty good, isn't it?" he said.

I nodded again.

"So how'd you like Ava?" he said.

I hesitated. I thought how I answered might mean life or death. I opened my eyes to see what kind of expression was on his face, to see if he looked angry, but I was immediately blinded by the spotlight so I shut my eyes again.

"I said how did you like Ava?" he said.

"Okay," I said.

"Just okay?" he said and I felt the forceps dig into my flesh a little. I jerked away.

"Is she okay, or is she better than okay?" he said.

"Better," I said.

"Is that all? Just better?" he said.

"More," I said.

"What?" he said. "The truth."

"When I saw her without her clothes on I was willing to do whatever I had to—anything—to be with her," I said. "I didn't care if I had to spend the rest of my life running from you. I know I messed up, but please don't do what you said you would. Please."

He kept working. *Ping. Ping.*

"You know, when I was a boy," he said, "never in my wildest dreams would I have seen myself sitting here like I am right now."

That caught me off guard, so it took me a moment to answer.

"Yeah, I guess the same goes for me," I said.

"How in hell did it happen?" he said.

"I don't know," I said.

Ping. Then I felt the forceps leave my flesh.

"No use thinking about it," he said.

"No," I said.

He started working on me again.

"Tell me about Tucson," he said.

So I started telling him about the college girl. He laughed a lot and asked a few questions, but I must've passed out while I was talking because I don't remember anything else until the next morning, when I woke up in Los Angeles City Hospital. No idea how I got there. First thing I did was grab between my legs—everything was there.

When I checked out three days later, there was a locked satchel with my name on it in the patient-valuable safe and inside it was fifty thousand dollars. I ended up with close to sixty thousand dollars for two months' work for Hughes.

I blew it all, every penny, within a year.

The Screening Room

On December 24, 1957—Howard Hughes's fifty-second birthday—he left the bungalow at the Beverly Hills Hotel that he shared with his wife of eleven months, Jean Peters, and had an aide drive him to a small screening room owned by a friend. The screening room was the size of a three-car garage and was in disrepair, with flaking white paint and a scratchy sound system. Two days earlier, Hughes had had the theater seats removed and replaced with a cheap red vinyl recliner, a small table beside it and a tall lamp behind it. A telephone was on the floor.

The night of his arrival Hughes sat down in the recliner with a bag of candy bars, stacked seven boxes of Kleenex on the table, and signaled for a film to start, *Blood and Sand,* a bullfighting melodrama starring his wife. He watched it three times in a row, tears running down his cheeks through most of the third showing. Then he signaled for Hitchcock's *Strangers on a Train* to start. When that ended, he watched *The Bridges at Toko-Ri* with William Holden.

Except to use the bathroom across the hall Hughes didn't leave this screening room for five months. Movies ran anywhere from eight to twelve hours a day, and during his stay he watched 317 different ones. He never changed clothes, and instead went naked when the clothes he had on that first night grew too filthy and tattered to wear. He never bathed. He ate nothing but candy bars and Texas pecans, and drank only milk. He did not allow anyone to speak to him, but instead made aides write their messages on yellow legal pads; he answered the same way. He was obsessed with germs to a greater degree than ever before; however, he would often urinate against the wall rather than make use of the bathroom across the hall. Once, when he was asleep in his chair, aides started to clean the room because they could no longer bear the stench; Hughes awoke and in a rage stopped them. Paradoxically, though, he would not touch any surface unless his hand was protected by several layers of Kleenex, and upon awakening he would usually spend anywhere from one to four hours cleaning the telephone with Kleenex. He sometimes made as many as seventy-five phone calls a day. But he never called Jean Peters; instead, with a series of letters hand-delivered to her by his aides, he led her to believe he was in a hospital in a secret location because he had a highly contagious mystery disease no doctor could identify or cure.

After Hughes left the screening room, he was never quite the same again. He almost never appeared in public and always conducted his business over the telephone or through proxies. The man of charm, ambition, and unparalleled accomplishment, was gone.

Alton Reece's second interview with Jean Peters

My bus arrives at the Houston Greyhound station just after two A.M. The station is on an access road in an older, industrial section of the city, and I start walking down this road, lugging my duffel. The only traffic I meet is a yellow low rider that passes me slowly, blasting music with Spanish lyrics, breaking the late-night silence of the deserted smokestack-and-chain-link landscape. Finally I come to a motel, a mom-and-pop affair with a yellow neon sign that says MOTE—the lights for the L and the word SHORE'S above it are burned out and they stand in dark silhouette against the starless city sky. The motel is three low one-story buildings arranged in a **U**. From the interior of the **U** I hear loud music and voices, a party. I find the entrance to the office at the end of the first building, a glass door with a collapsible metal gate pulled across it, beside it a glass-and-mesh window with a speaking grate and under it a revolving tray. There's no light in the office, but I find an unmarked doorbell button and push it, which produces a muted buzz. No one appears. I push the buzzer again, and then again. Finally, a light comes on inside, and a moment later a young man appears, bleary-eyed, wearing a light blue jersey with 13 on it and blue gym shorts with white piping—he has an erection pushing at his shorts but he seems completely unself-conscious about it. He doesn't ask what I want, but just stares at me sullenly. I ask what a room costs and he mumbles thirty-five plus tax. I tell him I only have thirty. He nods, and revolves the empty tray so I can put my money in the well. I drop the bills, he revolves the tray, then revolves it again and in the well there's a key. Then he turns around and disappears through a doorway. A moment later, the light goes out.

I find my room, check the bed linens, and take the fitted sheet off the mattress because it's stained. Then I shower for the first time in three days, though there's no soap provided, no towels. I lay naked on the bare, musty-smelling mattress until I dry off. There's no air-conditioning, and when I check the television I find only two channels and these are wavy. Outside, the party sounds as if it's spilling into the courtyard parking lot, voices in both English and Spanish, Southern rock music twenty years out of date, and some strange popping sounds I can't identify. Finally, I fall into a hot, fitful sleep.

I awaken early, unrested, drenched in sweat, with a slight headache. I take another shower, dry myself with the bedspread, then dress and leave.

I don't have a watch, but I know I walk at least an hour, until finally I reach a business district with office buildings and coffee stands. I see a bank clock that says it's 8:17. I sit down on a bench near a coffee stand and a pay phone, and wait until the bank clock says it's nine before I call Jean Peters on the pay phone and ask if it's convenient for her to see me today, I have a couple of things I need to ask her about. After a moment's hesitation, she says yes, but give her an hour, then, no, make it an hour and a half.

I use the last of my money for bus fare. The nearest bus stop to Jean Peters's affluent neighborhood is still a twenty-minute walk away, and the route I have to take is a busy four-lane with no sidewalks and a very narrow shoulder. Each moment it seems as if I'll be hit by oncoming traffic, and more than a few impatient drivers blow their horns when they have to swerve a bit to avoid me. By the time I reach the guardhouse at the gate to Jean Peters's community my clothes are drenched in sweat. The guard steps out of his hut and brusquely asks what I want—it's a different guard than last time, a young, bulky Samoan, his billed officer's hat too small for him, perched on the crown of his head comically, like a beanie, looking as if the slightest breeze would knock it off. I tell him my name and who I'm there to see. He reaches into the door of the hut for a clipboard, examines the top page, then the page under it, and says, You're supposed to be in a 1985 Ford station wagon. Well, I say, the

*last time I was. Yeah, then where is it? he says, smirking, obviously
taking pleasure in the petty power he's exercising. I start to argue with
him, then remember that all I want is to get past him, so I smile and
say I sold the car. That right? he says. Huh. Well, let me call Miss
Peters and see what she thinks.*

*It takes me another ten minutes to walk to Jean Peters's con-
dominium. H. L. Landry's dark blue Cadillac is parked in her
driveway. When I ring the bell, the door opens almost immediately.
Jean Peters greets me, does a quick double take she tries to hide, then in
her gracious way says it's good to see me again. She's walking without a
cane now, though she still has a slight limp. H. L. Landry is in the living
room watching television. He gets up from the couch and comes out to the
hallway to shake my hand. Then Jean Peters and I go down the hall
to the breakfast nook, and she reminds me that our original agreement
about our interview is still in effect. I say there's a small problem with
that, the batteries in my recorder are dead. She asks what type I need,
then goes into the kitchen and opens a drawer, rummages through it,
and pulls out an unopened pack of triple A's and brings it to the table.
I thank her, load the batteries, and we begin the interview.*

AR: Boy, it's really nice to be somewhere where it's cool. It
    seems like I've been walking all morning.
JP: Would you like some water?
AR: If it's not too much trouble.
*(She gets up and fills a glass of water at the refrigerator dispenser and
brings it back to the table.)*
JP: There. Now, Alton, what did you want to see me about?
AR: *(I drink.)* I have this letter. *(I lean over and unzip my duffel
    and rummage until I find the letter, then hand it to her.)* I believe

you wrote that to Hughes when he disappeared at the end of nineteen-fifty-seven, when he went to the screening room in Hollywood for five months.

JP: *(Looking over the letter.)* Yes, I wrote this.

AR: If you want to keep it, you're welcome to. I have a copy.

JP: No, I have no use for it. *(She pushes it back across the table.)*

AR: What I was hoping was that you might have some of the letters Hughes wrote to you during that time.

JP: *(She considers.)* Well, I do have a lot of Howard's correspondence, and there could be some letters from that time. I suppose I can check. He wrote me a lot during that period, but most of them were so painful to read I just threw them away. *(She stares out the window a moment, then she shakes her head, pushes her chair away from the table and stands up.)* If I do have any of those letters, though, you understand that I can't let you take them, don't you? You'll have to copy them. You can use my computer to type them, if you want.

AR: That's fine.

(She starts down the hallway that leads into the back of the condo.)

AR: Mrs. Peters?

JP: *(Stopping.)* Yes?

AR: Do you have an Internet connection?

JP: Yes.

AR: Would it be okay if I got on-line while you're looking for those letters? I need to check my email. I'd really appreciate it.

JP: Yes, all right. Come on.

(I follow her down the hallway. There are four closed doors on the hallway, one at the end, two on one side and one on the other.

She stops at the first door on the side that has two doors and opens it.)

JP: It's already on, all you have to do is turn on the monitor.
Just click on the ISP icon. The password's stored.

AR: Thank you.

(She leaves the door open when she leaves, and then heads back toward the kitchen. A moment later, she passes the doorway again going down the hall, and then H. L. Landry appears in the doorway of the room I'm in. He nods at me, then just stands in the doorway with his hands behind his back, watching me. I sit down at the computer, which is on an antique oak table positioned against the wall opposite the door. The table is cluttered, has papers scattered on it, knickknacks, framed photos, a green-shaded railroad lamp. I switch on the lamp, turn on the monitor, and use the mouse to start the connection. While I'm waiting for the connection to complete I glance at the papers on the desk, the knickknacks—there's a little glass dome that "snows," only it's a beach scene, and a small gold horse three inches high and four inches long, studded with what look like real rubies for eyes and on the saddle tiny pale green stones that look like emeralds.

My email has 114 messages. There's only one from my wife and it's almost six weeks old; I count eight from my editor, three from my agent, nineteen from Lisa Trundle, two from my lawyer, three from the Hughes Archives, a total of twenty-seven from my three assistants. I open the message from my wife first and begin reading, but before I'm halfway through it I stop and hit Delete. Then I keep deleting unopened messages until the inbox is empty.)

JP: *(Calling from across the hall.)* H. L.?

HL: Yes?

JP: Could you come help me get this box down out of the closet?

HL: Certainly.

(I glance over my shoulder and see that he's gone, then pick up the gold horse and put it in my pants pocket. Then I stare out the window behind the computer at a sapling in the yard braced with two lengths of twine. On one of its thin, leafless branches a bird with a gray body and a dark blue chest cocks its head back and forth. I keep watching it. Then I feel a tap on my shoulder, and when I turn my head H. L. Landry is standing behind me.)

HL: Jean wanted you to have this. *(He holds out a thin rectangle of bills folded in half.)* She doesn't want to make a federal case out of this, though, so there's no need to say anything to her. She knows you appreciate it, and she knows you'll repay her later.

AR: I couldn't.

HL: She insists. *(He reaches out and takes my hand and presses the bills into my palm. I nod, stick the money in my shirt pocket, then swivel the chair around and stare out the window again. The bird cocks its head back and forth, up and down. Then suddenly it flies away. Not long after that, Jean Peters enters the room.)*

JP: I found one.

(She hands me the letter. The paper is from an oversized yellow legal pad and is brittle with age. The handwriting sprawls and leans down the page, nothing like Hughes's usually neat script, but the signature at the bottom is without question his.)

AR: This is just what I was looking for. Thanks.

(Jean Peters and H. L. Landry watch as I type the short letter and

print out a copy. When I'm finished, I turn off the monitor and stand up and face the two of them.)

JP: Well, all right, Alton. It's been good to see you again.

AR: Yes, and thank you for everything.

Jean Peters letter, January 27, 1958

Dear Howard,

Your letters over the last two weeks have led me to believe the medication they are giving you is quite strong. You don't seem quite yourself and that is why I have not written until now. But even now I don't really know what to say. I am not betraying you. I am here and willing to be the best wife I know how to be for you. Why can't you believe that? I miss you more than I can say, and I am worried sick about you. If you believe anything, believe that. I love you and want to be with you more than anything in the world. Please believe that, too.

Where is your hospital? Howard, tell me where you are. Let me come help nurse you back to health.

I love you,

Jean

Hughes letter, February 1, 1958

Dear Jean,

If you cook the potatoes in tap water you might as well go ahead and blow your brains out. Boiling does not 100%

sterilize the tap water—ask any scientist worth his salt. For the love of God cook them in hot oil.

I'm coming home soon. I'm going to take care of you. We're going to be together. Watch for me.

Love,

Howard

A NOTE ON THE TYPE

The text of this book is set in Bembo, the original
types for which were cut by Francesco Griffo for the
Venetian printer Aldus Manutius, and were first used in
1495 for Cardinal Bembo's *De Aetna*. Claude Garamond
(1480–1561) used Bembo as a model, and so it became
the front runner of standard European type for the
following two centuries. Its modern form was designed,
following the original, for Monotype in 1929 and is
widely in use today.